Also available by Pete Johnson, and
published by Corgi Yearling Books:

THE GHOST DOG
*Winner of the 1997 Young Telegraph/
Fully Booked Award*
'Incredibly enjoyable' BOOKS FOR KEEPS

MY FRIEND'S A WEREWOLF
'Will make any reader stop and think'
THE SCHOOL LIBRARIAN

THE PHANTOM THIEF
'A dynamic writer'
NATIONAL ASSOCIATION FOR
TEACHING ENGLISH

# Eyes of the Alien

## Pete Johnson

*Illustrated by David Wyatt*

CORGI YEARLING BOOKS

EYES OF THE ALIEN
A CORGI YEARLING BOOK : 0 440 86390 2

First publication in Great Britain

PRINTING HISTORY
Corgi Yearling edition published 1999

5 7 9 10 8 6

Typeset by
Phoenix Typesetting, Ilkley, West Yorkshire.

Corgi Yearling Books are published by Random House Children's Books,
61–63 Uxbridge Road, London W5 5SA,
a division of The Random House Group Ltd,
in Australia by Random House Australia (Pty) Ltd,
20 Alfred Street, Milsons Point, Sydney, NSW 2061, Australia,
in New Zealand by Random House New Zealand Ltd,
18 Poland Road, Glenfield, Auckland 10, New Zealand
and in South Africa by Random House (Pty) Ltd,
Endulini, 5a Jubilee Road, Parktown 2193, South Africa.

Made and printed in Great Britain by
Cox & Wyman Ltd, Reading, Berkshire.

*This is the most amazing story you will ever read. And we didn't want to miss out a single detail. So that's why two of us are telling you the story.*

Sam(antha)   and Freddie

# CHAPTER ONE
## by Sam

It all started the afternoon I fell off my bike and knocked myself out.

I was having a bike race with Freddie in Bray Wood – I was right out in the lead too – when I hit something.

Freddie found me lying 'horribly still' and charged off to get help.

The next thing I remember is trying to open my eyes, only they stung, because some dust had got into them. So everything was blurred. No-one was about, yet I sensed someone was nearby. Then I saw this figure a little way from me.

I could only see this figure very dimly. But it was a man and he was wearing a dark suit and a large hat. He didn't move any closer. He just stood there looking at me. I wondered who he was. He was dressed very strangely for a walk in the woods. He looked like a kind of businessman. Then I had this mad idea he was an undertaker waiting for his next customer: me.

He just made me feel so uneasy, especially the way he seemed to be observing me, as if I were a rare animal he'd just discovered.

Then, to my great relief someone else swam into view: Miss West, who's both my teacher and my Aunt Margaret. She was the first person Freddie had found. And when he told her about the accident he said she rushed off to help me faster than the wind. That made me feel a bit ashamed as earlier that day she and I had had a massive row.

My aunt had lived abroad for years and I only met up with her recently. Now she was moving away and wanted me to go with her, while I wanted to stay with my foster parents (Uncle Tony and Auntie Judy). She made such a fuss about it. I remember her face turned scalding red. I think I must have really upset her.

Anyway, I was so relieved to see her I passed out again. The next time I looked up there was a small crowd around me, including Aunt Margaret and Freddie. (He said my eyes were rolling about in my head and I looked extremely weird, still, he would.)

But the man had gone. And afterwards when I asked Aunt Margaret about him she denied he'd ever existed. She insisted no man had been there when she arrived. But she was wrong. She'd stood right next to him.

I thought that was so odd and told Freddie. We talked about it for ages. But then I might have forgotten the whole thing if I hadn't seen the man again in the most horrible way.

It was a week later. I was at home, still convalescing. I'd felt tired that afternoon (even though I hadn't really done anything) so I went to bed and had a nap. I'd hardly closed my eyes when I was back at the scene of the accident. I was lying on the ground like before. And he was there again. Now I could see him a little more clearly. His dark grey suit had wide lapels and looked very old-fashioned and his hat was pulled right down over his face.

But this time he raised his head and I glimpsed his eyes: huge eyes that were so black they hid everything. You could never see inside those eyes. And what was really weird: his eyes didn't seem to have any pupils.

Then he whispered my name. 'Samantha.' That gave me the shock of my life. How did he know who I was?

He said my name again: 'Samantha.'

I didn't answer, didn't move. I was terrified. How can you tell someone is an enemy when they've only said one word? You just know, don't you? A kind of intuition I suppose. And right then I knew he was to be feared, always.

'Leave me alone,' I cried.

Next moment I was back at home again. I nearly cried with relief. I hardly ever get nightmares and afterwards I can only remember little pieces of them. But this nightmare (or afternoonmare) was different. I couldn't seem to come out of it. It kept racing through my head.

Perhaps if I could talk to someone the dream would fade away. I called out to Auntie Judy. But she wasn't back from the shops yet. I looked at my watch. Just gone half past three. Freddie would be home from school soon. How I wished he was here now. Everything was too still and quiet.

The only noise was the rain hissing against the window. It seemed to be softly whispering my name . . . Sam, Sam, Sam.

Then came another sound.

Someone was pounding on the front door.

I shot up in bed. 'Who is it?' I quavered.

Silence again.

Slowly, fearfully, I began to creep downstairs. Half-way down the stairs you can see the front door. We've got this pebbled glass, so it's like looking through one of those distorting mirrors you get at fairgrounds. But at least it gives you some idea who's there.

Someone was there now all right.

I edged down a couple more steps. The face seemed to be right up against the glass. I couldn't see it very clearly. But I recognized those huge black eyes staring in at me.

Then I screamed.

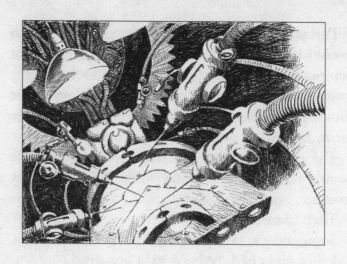

# CHAPTER TWO
## by Freddie

I just laughed at first.

I was only fooling about. We'd been looking at space travel and aliens in Miss West's class – the first interesting lesson we'd ever had with her – then she asked me, as I knew a lot about aliens, if I'd dress up as one the day after tomorrow, and then the class could ask me questions.

So, after school, I bought this cheap little mask. You know the kind: light-bulb head, huge wrap-about eyes, slit for a mouth, light grey skin. Mine also had a silver bolt through its neck. A kind of

Frankenstein alien. But it was still a bit plain. I'd have liked it to have had some warts, at least. It was too tame to be scary, in daylight anyhow.

I was walking home in the mask when I met Auntie Judy. She was fumbling about for her key. So I rapped on the door, peered in to see where Sam was, and she screamed the house down.

No, I'm exaggerating a bit now. It was just one scream. Still, it was pretty loud, and Sam was dead embarrassed afterwards.

Auntie Judy tried to make it better by saying, 'Seeing that mask through pebbled glass would be enough to scare anyone.' But she was just making Sam feel worse. I could tell.

'It wasn't the mask,' explained Sam. 'It was just the man I saw when I had that accident turned up in my dream a few minutes ago and he had these huge black eyes without any pupils.'

'Alien eyes,' I said.

'And he was looking at me in this really menacing way; he even knew my name. Then I woke up and went downstairs and saw those same eyes staring in at me . . .'

'Just an unfortunate coincidence then,' said Auntie Judy. 'It's such a shame you had the bad dream when you were on your own. It takes longer to snap back into real life then, doesn't it?'

Sam nodded. I was sure that dream was still running through her head.

Then Miss West came round. Since the accident she's turned up every day to check on Sam. And every day she'll have a cup of tea and one digestive biscuit. It was starting to really bug me.

'Miss West,' I said, 'why don't you let your hair down today and have a custard cream instead?'

Miss West gave me one of her spray-on smiles, and took one digestive biscuit.

By the way, she thinks I'm a complete cod. Still, I'm not exactly her biggest fan either. I wouldn't say she's a bad teacher: she certainly knows a lot and she loves explaining things in her high, sing-song voice. But she's deadly serious all the time. You can never have a laugh with her, and she's very strict. If you do one thing wrong she gives you this really evil stare. No-one likes her.

Sam started telling Miss West about her nightmare. Auntie Judy was getting a bit concerned. I think she was worried about Sam upsetting herself

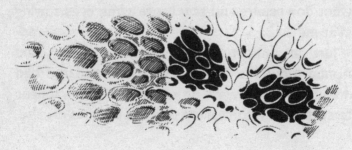

again. But Miss West seemed surprisingly inter-
ested until Sam said the man was 'someone quite
bad and scary'. Then she clicked her tongue with
irritation.

I thought that was a bit cheeky. So I chipped in,
'Actually, Miss West, the man in Sam's dream is just
like the one she saw straight after her accident. The
one who was standing right next to you. The one
you don't remember now.'

'I don't remember him, Freddie,' replied Miss
West in her slow, patronizing voice, 'because no
man of that description was ever there.' Auntie
Judy gave me a warning glance: rudeness was something she wouldn't allow. So I fled upstairs to my
room.

I felt sorry for Sam. It was bad enough having Miss
West for a teacher, I'd go crazy if she was my aunt.
What's worse, she's the only relation Sam's got.
Her parents died in a car accident shortly after Sam
was born. She can hardly remember either of them.
She's got this picture of them on her dressing-table.
They look really nice: nothing like Miss West.

She hardly saw Miss West until she was fostered
by Auntie Judy and Uncle Tony in January, six
months ago now. Then Miss West turned up. Talk
about bad timing.

Actually, Sam had quite a hard time when she

joined my class. It was partly because of Miss West being her aunt. But also because Sam was very quiet, very brainy (she comes top in just about everything), and a bit too keen, if you know what I mean.

First one girl began picking on Sam, then they all joined in. One day, I remember, these girls were talking about their mums and dads, then one of them said to Sam: 'Oh, sorry, you don't know what we're talking about, do you?'

Sam's eyes filled with tears. Big mistake, as I told her afterwards.

I explained: they think you're a loser because you haven't got any parents so you've got to show them that you're not. And the first rule, never let them see when they've got to you.

I know what I'm talking about. I used to get picked on because my parents weren't around and also, because when I was six, all my hair fell out.

What happened was, I was staying with this couple and I didn't get on with them at all. I was always in the wrong and one day it just got to me. So I decided I was going to run away and make myself a tree-house and live up there for ever. I was only six, remember.

I climbed up really high as well, until I lost my balance and tumbled to the ground, face first. I wasn't too badly hurt but I'd damaged this nerve on my lip. I wasn't very bothered about that, until a few days later I woke up to find my pillow covered in hair.

I thought that someone must have crept in and scalped me in the night. But no, my hair had all fallen out just like that. And it seems there's not much chance of it growing back, ever. Still, think of all the money I'm saving on shampoos.

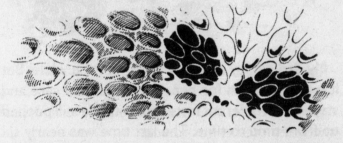

For a while I wore hats all the time. Now I don't bother. Of course I still get the jokes: I'll be walking down the street, minding my own business, when someone will call out 'Hello baldilocks'. I mean, how original. But as I say, you must never get mad, just laugh it off and say something like 'Yeah, I knew I shouldn't have washed my hair in acid rain'.

You're probably wondering what happened to my mum and dad. It's all right, you can ask. My mum's still around somewhere. She was already married when she had me 'by accident'. And afterwards she went back to her family again. I suppose you can't blame her. She had five children already, so she probably needed another one like a hole in the head.

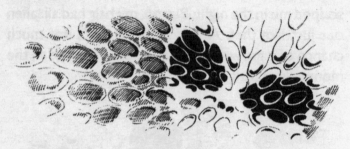

My dad did try and look after me for a while. But it was too much for him. So I went into care and stayed with different foster parents. He still popped up from time to time. The last time was nearly six years ago. He bought me this Arsenal coat. I've still got it. I remember, we went on a bus into town and I pretended the bus was a spacecraft (sad but true). I haven't seen him since. He left this country in search of work. He sends me the odd card and present. But that's all.

And I've stayed in some dodgy places, I can tell you. One time I woke up to find what looked like giant dandruff on my pillow. Wow, I thought, I might not have any hair but I've still got very impressive dandruff. But it turned out the room was so damp that clumps of plaster were falling off the ceiling while I was asleep.

I've been moved about so often. One time I over-heard this man say about me: 'The boy has been lost in the system.' Well, the only system I knew was the *solar* system. Did he mean when I was born I'd fallen from the stars, and really, I was an alien? I quite liked the idea. After all, aliens can go anywhere, can't they? I wouldn't mind a trip or two around the galaxy.

I'm fascinated by extra-terrestrials: it started when I began collecting these little plastic models – I've got over fifty of them now, all lined up on my shelf. And wherever I go the aliens go too. They arrived here with me on March 11th last year. And we still haven't been chucked out. Amazing.

There's such a good atmosphere here. As soon as you walk in, this house just wraps itself around you. Sean, who's been here three years, says exactly the same.

Uncle Tony and Auntie Judy can be quite strict. I mean, they just hate it if you leave your things downstairs at night, and they're a bit over-keen about keeping your bedroom tidy. But that's cool. We've all got our hang-ups. And at least they don't keep on telling me to 'shut up' or 'stop being so lippy'. Actually, they're just about the only people in the universe who've never said that to me.

Anyway, Miss West finally left, and Sam escaped upstairs. She slumped onto the chair in my bedroom.

'Had a nice cosy chat with your old peculiar?' I asked.

'Oh, it was just lovely,' said Sam, closing her eyes.

'I'd better take my mask away,' I added, teasingly, 'before you see it and scream again.'

Sam's eyes flew open. 'The man in my dream had eyes exactly like that, you know.' She pointed at my mask.

'Then your nightmare man is obviously an alien who's got into your dreams and is trying to hypnotize you so he can abduct you, and do experiments on you with massive needles.'

I was just fooling about really, but Sam wasn't smiling.

'Hey, Sam, maybe you've been experimented on and don't even remember.' I leapt forward and peered up her nose.

'What are you doing?' she cried.

'Just checking. Usually if you've been experimented on you find some tinfoil up your nose afterwards. But you're all right, just the usual bogies.'

She still didn't smile. 'Freddie, do you really think

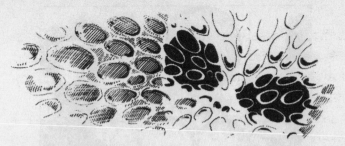

he could be an alien? I mean, when I had my accident he was there, just studying me. Why won't my
aunt admit that?'

I stopped teasing her. 'Maybe because she really
didn't see him. Look, you knocked yourself out and
when you came round you thought you saw an
eerie, shadowy figure with alien eyes. Today you
had a little dream about him. I'd say he only lives
inside your head.'

'Oh, would you?' She sounded both surprised and
relieved.

'After an accident weird things can happen in
your head – or on it.' I tapped my own head, and
grinned. At last she began to smile as well.

Then we forgot about E.T.s as Auntie Judy rushed
in with some very surprising news. She'd just been
chatting on the phone with my dad, of all people.
He was back in this country and wanted to see me
– tomorrow night.

# CHAPTER THREE
## by Sam

It was really exciting: Freddie's dad turning up out of the blue after all these years and inviting Freddie out for a meal.

Freddie asked me to come to the meal too. I was surprised he wanted me there. But he said he hadn't seen his dad since 1066, so if the conversation went a bit dead he could always chat to me instead.

So we both got ready to go out. Only the bathroom was permanently engaged.

'Freddie, what are you doing in there?' I called.

'Unravelling secret microfilm in the sink. What do you think?'

The bathroom door finally sprung open. 'What a pong,' I cried. Freddie must have splashed on half a gallon of Sean's aftershave. He had on his best clothes too. I knew he really wanted to impress his dad.

I kept imagining their reunion. They'd run up to each other, they'd smile shyly, then they'd have this massive hug and wouldn't want to let go of each other. I was so happy for Freddie – but I couldn't help feeling a bit sad for myself too. Tonight reminded me I'd never ever see my own parents again.

We sat on the stairs, waiting. Auntie Judy kept telling us to come into the kitchen. But Freddie wouldn't budge. Seven o'clock passed. I was surprised Freddie's dad was late. If I was going to see my son after all this time I wouldn't have been late.

Freddie had been really worked up. Now he started to go quiet. So did I. Then came the phone call. I couldn't hear much but I guessed. Uncle Tony came and told us. He said, 'It's a great shame, I know, but your dad genuinely can't make it, Freddie. He's so disappointed. But there'll be other times soon.'

I felt so angry. Why couldn't Freddie's dad make it? What was more important than seeing his own son?

Freddie just said 'OK' really softly, and disappeared upstairs. Auntie Judy said it was best to leave him alone for a while. I wasn't so sure. I went to ask Sean, who was sitting in the kitchen doing his homework. Sean is fifteen and gets on well with Freddie even though he's always calling him 'a mad boy'.

Sean considered. 'Yeah, perhaps he is best on his own for now,' then he clenched up his hands into fists. 'Parents are always bottling out, you know . . . it's happened a few times here, to him for instance.'

He started pointing at the photos on the wall. Auntie Judy and Uncle Tony haven't got any children of their own, but they've fostered eleven of us over the years. They're all up on the wall with their latest ones – Sean, Freddie and me – right in the centre.

My eyes were caught by one boy with big starey eyes. He was the only person on the wall not smiling. He looked so miserable and totally lost.

'Did you know him?' I asked, pointing.

'Oh yeah,' replied Sean. 'He was called Arnold. He was really shy, used to walk around staring at the ground all the time. He didn't fit in here at all, did he, Auntie Judy?'

Auntie Judy came over. 'No,' she said. 'He didn't, poor chap. Our only failure.'

'What happened to him?' I asked.

'I'm not sure exactly. We still get the odd report about him, and he's happier now . . . at least I hope he is.'

It was my turn to set the table. I'd set a place for Freddie even though no-one was expecting him to come down. But he did, reeking of aftershave and wearing his alien mask.

'Ah, here's Freddie, just in time for my spaghetti Bolognese special, made from whatever's in the fridge,' said Uncle Tony.

'How are you feeling, love?' asked Auntie Judy. Everyone was staring at Freddie. We all felt so sorry for him but I don't think anyone knew exactly what to say.

Freddie put on this high-pitched, squeaky voice and replied, 'I'm sorry, I'm from another planet so I do not speak your language very well . . . Excuse me, kindly.'

We all laughed as if Freddie had just made the funniest joke in the world.

'So what planet are you from, exactly?' asked Sean.

'The planet Helium,' replied Freddie, his voice even more high-pitched.

We laughed again. Then we started eating. Only the mouthpiece of Freddie's mask was very small. Soon bits of Bolognese were dangling down his chin.

'Freddie, you're losing all of your food,' said Uncle Tony.

He didn't answer.

Uncle Tony half-closed his eyes, a sure sign he was getting cross. 'Take that mask off before you put everyone off their meal.'

Freddie looked up. 'On my planet it is good manners to leave food behind on your face. It means you have enjoyed the meal.'

Normally, Auntie Judy and Uncle Tony wouldn't have allowed him to get away with that. But today, Uncle Tony just half-closed his eyes again while Auntie Judy jumped up to get Freddie a large straw.

After we'd finished Uncle Tony said, 'Shall we adjourn to the den?' Uncle Tony had converted the garage into a room where, as he put it, we could always 'chill out'. 'How about a game of table football?' he went on. 'Me and Sam against Freddie and Sean. We'll beat them easily.'

'Not a chance,' said Sean.

He turned to Freddie, who shrugged his shoulders. 'I'm sorry, but what is table football?' he asked.

We were all a bit stunned by that question because table football is a great favourite of Freddie's. Usually he's the one trying to persuade us to play with him.

'Come on, Freddie, we'll be the red side,' began Sean, coaxingly. (He and Freddie both support Arsenal.)

'Sorry, I do not know what the red side is,' declared Freddie. He got up. 'Thank you for the pleasure of my company. Goodbye.'

'Safe journey home,' Sean called after him.

Freddie didn't come out of his room for the rest of the evening. I went to bed early as I was going back to school tomorrow. But first I tapped on my wall, twice. Freddie's in the room next to mine and we have this little code: two taps means 'come in, I want to talk to you'. Freddie didn't answer. He could have been asleep. But I don't think he was.

It took me ages to fall asleep. I was nervous about what nightmares might be waiting for me. Finally, I drifted off. Then I heard a voice whispering my name. I stirred.

'Sam, Sam.'

Now the voice was really close. I squinted my eyes open. The darkness shifted to reveal something even darker: two huge eyes staring right at me. A cry of terror rose in my throat.

Then a familiar voice said, 'I couldn't sleep, and now neither can you.'

'Freddie,' I hissed. I could begin to see him now. He was standing by my desk in the corner, still in his mask.

'That's twice I've scared you in two days,' he said.

'Do you know what time it is?'

'Yes I do, thanks. Would you like to test me?'

'Test you?'

'You know I'm being an alien at school tomorrow. Well, I've got some questions here which you could ask me, as a kind of rehearsal. But only if you want to.'

I rubbed my eyes. 'You're mad.'

'No, I'm not mad, just very eccentric,' he corrected.

Then I remembered about his dad not turning up

tonight. I wanted to say something but I felt awkward as well. 'Shame your dad couldn't make it tonight,' I whispered at last.

Freddie stood completely still, not moving a muscle. 'It's his loss,' he said. Then he pressed the questions into my hand.

I switched on the bedside light. 'Your writing's terrible,' I muttered. 'All right, question one: do aliens abduct people?'

Freddie started pacing around my bedroom. 'Yes we do, but only because we need to find out about humans. It's just the same as when you humans go to the Amazonian rain forests and bring back some rare species to examine. We're only doing the same thing. We get you to lie on a medical table, shine a bright light on to you and take some samples of your hair, your fingernails, and ear-wax.'

'Ear-wax,' I repeated.

'Oh, yes, E.T.s are mad keen about ear-wax.'

'How do you know that?'

29

He laughed. 'I just do. It's in all the books on them. I've just been reading about being abducted. Did you know that the hours between one and three in the morning are the most common time for abductions. Imagine being wakened in the middle of the night to see alien eyes gazing at you . . .'

'I know exactly what that feels like,' I replied.

Freddie laughed again. 'Sometimes weird things happen before an abduction takes place, other times they just strike out of the blue. It must be so fascinating.'

'That's one word for it.'

'But,' he stopped pacing about, 'just think, you're lying in bed – another boring night – then suddenly, little green men or whatever appear, you're lifted out of bed, taken out of your home and out on to a flying saucer. They bring you back afterwards, of course. Only, if they really like you they invite you to live on their planet.'

'I didn't know that.'

'Yeah, they have this kind of zoo I suppose you'd call it, only this time the human beings are inside, being stared at by all the extra-terrestrials.'

'I'd hate that,' I said.

'I wouldn't.' Freddie stared into the dim light. 'So whenever they want to abduct me . . .'

'You don't mean that.'

'I do, Sam,' his voice rose. 'And I wouldn't care if I never came back. I really wouldn't.'

He sounded so miserable and sad my heart went out to him. Then I felt a rush of fear as well. 'You mustn't say that,' I whispered.

'Why, are you afraid they might hear?'

'No, of course not. It's only, that . . . I don't know really,' I began. And I didn't, I just knew icy chills were suddenly running through me.

'Well, I hope they do come for me,' cried Freddie. 'So if any aliens are ear-wigging . . . I'll be waiting, all right.'

# CHAPTER FOUR
### by Freddie

So there I was, perched on Miss West's desk wearing my alien mask, a white shiny top (once in a galaxy far away Uncle Tony had worn that to discos), and creamy white trousers. Oh yes, I also had webbed hands.

To be honest, I still didn't look much like an alien. In fact, anyone else in those clothes would have looked a right munchkin.

But I played the part with such conviction people began to believe me, a little bit anyhow. Now I know how actors must feel. It's a totally amazing feeling.

It started off with Sam asking me the questions

we'd rehearsed. That went pretty well. Then Sam said the class could cross-examine the 'special guest alien' (that's how Sam introduced me – I liked it). And at first I got silly questions such as, 'Alien, what planet do you buy your clothes from?' I immediately snapped back, 'From the planet "No Taste" and it's Mr Alien to you.' That got a big laugh. But then they started asking me about abductions.

Finally, one humanoid (and that's how I was starting to see them now), called out, 'I don't think you've got any right to abduct people.' There were loud murmurs of agreement.

'I'm sorry, but I disagree,' I replied. 'We want to help you – and goodness knows you humanoids need help. But we can only do that by observing and experimenting on you. Yet we try and not scare you too much. We always give you a tour of the spaceship afterwards. And we take you home safely. Well, usually we do. Still . . .' I pointed at a humanoid at the back who gets into nearly as much trouble as me, 'I think if we kept *you* on my planet we'd be doing everyone here a big favour.'

They all laughed at that. Amazingly, even Miss West's lips twitched. I decided it must be her birthday – or she'd got a new boyfriend. She only turned frosty again when someone asked me how I went to the toilet.

'You're getting silly now,' she said.

But I could have answered that one too. I was so into the part you could have asked me anything and I'd have ad-libbed a reply. I was on such a roll. Anyway, the bell went and everyone flocked round congratulating me. It's never happened to me before. People have smirked at my jokes and stuff. But today was different. Today, I was the business. That's why I couldn't bring myself to take the mask off.

Miss West asked Sam and me to stay behind for a minute. 'A most pleasing effort, Freddie. For once you controlled all your inappropriate impulses.'

Wow, Miss West was saying something nice to me, I think. I was surprised all her teeth didn't fall out with the shock.

'And Sam, what did you think of Freddie's performance as an alien?'

'I thought he was totally brilliant.'

For just a second I thought Miss West looked

disappointed. What else was she expecting Sam to say? But then she went on, 'And how are you feeling, Sam – not too tired?'

'No, I'm fine.'

'Good, well I can't come round and see you tonight as I'm expecting some visitors.' I watched Sam trying to look grief-stricken at this news. 'By the way, Sam, you haven't had any more night-mares, have you?'

'No, thank goodness.'

'Well, when you do, let me know at once, won't you?' Then she gave a rather peculiar smile. 'I mean, if you do, of course.'

Back home Uncle Tony was going away on a business trip for a few days. Sam and I helped him pack – and told him about my performance as an E.T. I'd changed into my usual clothes now but I was still wearing the mask.

As Uncle Tony was leaving I heard him whisper to Auntie Judy, 'Any emergencies, call me at once, all right.'

I smiled to myself. What emergencies was he expecting? Adults have to make such a big deal of everything, don't they?

Later that evening Sean went round a friend's house; Auntie Judy, Sam and me were playing cards in the den when the phone rang.

'What's he forgotten this time?' muttered Auntie Judy.

But it wasn't Uncle Tony.

The call was for me. It was my dad. When Auntie Judy told me, I could only stare at her, as if all my batteries had suddenly run out.

Sam has explained what happened last night. I'll just tell you, when my dad called me right out of the blue and said he wanted to see me, I was dead excited. And when for no good reason he didn't turn up he hurt me a lot. Now, here he was again. But this time I wasn't excited or hurt. I was just plain mad.

He had no right to mess me about like this. I wasn't some sort of toy he could play with when he was feeling a bit bored. He'd been a rotten dad anyhow. And I didn't want anything to do with him.

That's exactly what I told Auntie Judy.

Auntie Judy's quite good at persuading me to do things. But today she didn't. She just said, 'Yes, all right, love.'

As soon as she'd gone I jumped to my feet. 'I'm getting out of here,' I said. My head was hammering furiously. 'Coming?'

'Yes, all right,' said Sam. 'But on one condition: you take that mask off first.'

Yes, I was still wearing it and I was feeling a bit argumentative as well. 'Why should I?'

'Because I hate talking to you when you're wearing that silly mask. I can't see your eyes and . . . it reminds me of my nightmare. All right?'

She was getting as worked up as me now. So I flung the mask on to the floor and cried, 'Happy now?' and sped out of the back door.

'What are you running for?' she asked. 'My leg still hurts, you know.'

I waited for her. Then we went across the road to the common. We made for the play area right over the other side of the common. We wouldn't go near this spot in the daytime. But at night it's different. No little kids playing there then. It's always deserted and feels kind of strange and spooky, so I feel right at home there.

If ever Sam and I want to chat about something private we sit at the top of the slide. We went there that evening. Above us the clouds were heavy and dark, there was the smell of thunder in the air. No-one was about, not even the usual dog-walkers.

And then . . . I remember everything about the next few moments. First off, Sam said: 'I think we're the last people left in the world.'

'What a terrible thought,' I replied.

We were both in slightly funny moods. I was being a bit off with her, but only because I didn't want her – or anyone else – dripping sympathy all over me because of my dad. I think she realized that.

A cold wind blew softly into my ears. It began to shake this crisp packet, pulling and tugging at it and, finally, sending it soaring right up into the air. The crisp packet started doing this weird little dance all on its own. It was funny to watch.

But then we saw something much more amazing.

Way up in the sky I spotted this really bright star. I didn't think I'd ever seen a star glow and shine like this one.

'Look at that!' I cried.

But Sam was already looking at it.

Just fooling about, I shouted out to the star, 'Hey, you're really skilful. Come a bit nearer.'

That's when it began to move.

'It's heard me,' I cried jokingly. Actually, I just thought it was a falling star. But it was hurtling in our direction at the most tremendous speed. And all the time it was getting brighter and brighter.

'It's not a star at all, is it?' cried Sam. 'It's too big. So what is it?'

'It's a spaceship full of aliens.'

We both laughed nervously.

## CHAPTER FIVE
*by Sam (and a bit by Freddie)*

I kept saying to myself that it has to be a plane. But there was no jet trail, no hum of engines, and surely it was moving too fast to be a plane. We just couldn't take our eyes off it.

Then, very suddenly, it stopped. It was as if it had hit an invisible barrier. And it just hung there in the air suspended right above the trees like a Christmas decoration (only it was June) at the other end of the common.

Freddie let out this cry. Then he put his hand up to his mouth as if to catch any further cries.

'What is it?' I whispered.

In reply, Freddie shot down the slide, staggered a few steps forward then grinned back at me. 'You know what it is, don't you? It's got to be a UFO, and we're seeing it. So come on.'

I followed him down the slide. My stomach was all knotted inside. I was dead scared and excited, and I couldn't help feeling a bit special too. To think Freddie and me had been singled out to see something as amazing as this. Well, of course we hadn't been singled out. We just happened to be in the right place at the right time, as they say.

But this was so incredible. I still couldn't believe it. Was it some kind of optical illusion which would vanish any second? But no, it continued to hover above us, glowing and shining with an unearthly brilliance. What exactly did it look like? I'd describe it as a dazzling ball of blue light, with a reddish glow around the edges. But it wasn't that big – roughly about the size of two flattened footballs – which made me wonder again if it could be a spacecraft.

Freddie nudged my arm. 'Look!'

'What?'

'Inside. There's someone inside there watching us.'

'Where?' I cried.

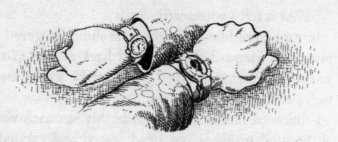

'Just there. It turned its face, it looked at me.'

My heart was pounding furiously. Were aliens about to confront us, forcing us into their craft? The air was tingling with danger now. I sensed something was about to happen.

Probably the aliens inside were sussing us out before they pounced. Animals do that, stop and sniff the air before they attack, don't they? I was getting more and more worked up, unsure whether to run away or what to do. But I have to admit, although I peered really hard I couldn't make out any aliens. I couldn't even see any windows. But Freddie did – so I'd better let him tell you the next bit.

FREDDIE: Yes, I definitely saw windows of some kind and inside there were two aliens. One I could see really clearly. He was staring out of the window at us. And he had those huge, dark alien eyes. The other one wasn't so clear. But he was there too.

There may have been others but I definitely saw two of them.

Now I know it sounds weird only me seeing them. But I felt as if for a few seconds my senses were magnified and I could really zoom in on that spacecraft. I'm not making any of this up, I swear. That's exactly what I saw. Now back to Sam.

SAM: Then something truly terrifying happened. The spacecraft suddenly moved. It swooped forward, skimming the trees as it did so, but still without making any sound at all.

'It's coming right for us,' cried Freddie, his breath hot on my neck. The next moment he yelled 'Down!' and we both fell onto the grass, just like soldiers do in those old war films when a shell is about to explode over their heads.

I'd fallen awkwardly and was gasping for air. I didn't dare sit up. Freddie was coughing beside me, making it seem more than ever as if we'd suddenly found ourselves in the trenches during a major battle.

Above me the cold air was suddenly turning much warmer. The spaceship was right on top of us. I could feel its heat on my back. I tried to look up, but the light was so bright I couldn't look at it for long. It was that very intense, sharp light you get from a photocopying machine or an X-ray. I lay there shaking, while the light seemed to cut right through me.

Something ran up my arms. It was like a chill, only it was warm. What was happening to us? I have never felt more scared.

The silence was suddenly broken by a high-pitched beeping noise, making me think of hospitals, operations, experiments. Soon aliens would be prodding me about, performing their tests on me. My body was shaking and twitching like a fish on the end of a giant line. And that's exactly how I felt.

Then all at once the light faded. I raised my head just in time to see the spacecraft shoot off into the sky like a bullet. In the twinkling of an eye it was gone. The sky was empty again. But the grass was stirring around me and there was still that beeping noise. On and on it went.

'Freddie,' I hissed.

He stirred, then he shook himself. He looked as if he had just woken up.

'It's gone,' I whispered.

'But that noise,' he gasped. Then he gave a strange kind of laugh. 'It's my watch. It must have set my alarm off.' He could hardly steady his hand as he switched the alarm off. Then he took several deep breaths. So did I. Sweat was running into my eyes. I brushed it away. My hands felt strange too. 'Have you got pins and needles in your hands?' asked Freddie.

'I think I've got them everywhere,' I replied.

We stumbled to our feet. My legs felt like water. There was just a dingy, dusty light. The wind whistled, and somewhere high in the trees a bird was calling. It sounded lonely and lost. We stood there, taking longer breaths now.

'What we just saw,' I began, 'what was it . . . exactly?'

'It was exactly an alien spacecraft,' replied Freddie. 'What I don't understand is . . . that alien ship seemed to be making straight for us, didn't it?'

I nodded.

'Like it could see us.'

I nodded again.

'Like it had picked us out.'

'But why would it do that?' I asked.

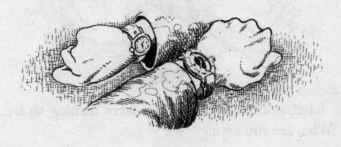

'I don't know, but it was after us all right – or one of us, anyhow.'

A moment later I said, 'Of course you did say you wanted to be abducted, didn't you? You said it only last night.'

His voice rose. 'And you reckon they heard me?'

I wasn't sure. I just knew I was very scared and if one of us had to be the alien's target I wanted it to be Freddie – not me. 'I'm only saying it's a bit of a coincidence.'

Freddie didn't reply. But his eyes were wide and staring. In the dim light he almost looked like an alien. Around us there was only the wind howling. The whole common seemed to be frozen with terror.

Then he said, slowly, 'Of course the weird thing is, the alien I saw in the spacecraft had huge, dark eyes . . . just like your nightmare man.'

I felt as though my insides were turning to ice. 'What are you saying?'

'Nothing.'

'Yes you are.'

'I'm just saying that the man you saw when you had your accident, and in your nightmare, was probably an alien . . . and then we see an alien spaceship. That's a bit of a coincidence too, isn't it?'

'But you said I imagined him, and he only lives inside my head.'

'Well, yeah . . .'

'So why are you saying something different now?'

'I'm not. I'm just saying it's a bit of a coincidence too . . .'

'I can't believe you're being so nasty,' I cried. Then something else occurred to me. 'And anyway, I never saw the aliens in the spacecraft – only you did.' I paused significantly.

Freddie's eyes were wider than ever now. 'OK, what do I care?' he whispered. 'Their spaceship can't be any worse than some of the places I've stayed at. They can abduct me any time. And if I'm gone in the morning, tell my dad he's missed his chance of seeing me for ever and not to expect a postcard, all right.'

Feeling a bit ashamed of my cowardice now, I whispered back, 'Freddie, you're not going anywhere. I won't let them take you.'

He smiled quickly, 'Let's get out of here.' He

squinted at his watch, then held it up to my ear. 'Mine's stopped. What's the time?'

I glanced down. 'Ten past nine.'

He waved his watch at me. 'Snap,' he said.

So both our watches had stopped. 'This often happens during sightings,' said Freddie. 'It's called the lost-time phenomenon. Later, people find out they've been away for hours. They don't remember what happened until they're put under hypnosis, then they discover they've been lying on a space-ship, with massive needles . . .'

'Thanks Freddie, I get the idea.' Then I said slowly, 'So we might have been experimented on and not even realize it.'

'That's right. We've got to find out what time it is.'

'It does seem very late, doesn't it?' I cried. And it had suddenly grown very dark.

'I reckon it's about midnight at least,' said Freddie. 'We'll have been missing for hours. People will be out searching for us.'

Right then, somewhere in the darkness, I heard our names being called.

# CHAPTER SIX
## by Freddie

I recognized Sean's voice rightaway. I called out to him. He came pounding out of the shadows. I was well pleased. In emergencies, Sean's someone you want around, even when he's saying, 'Freddie, you're a dead man. Auntie Judy's furious with you.'

Normally I'd have pointed out it wasn't just me who'd run off, Sam had gone as well. (Everyone always assumes I'm the ring-leader, but then I usually am.) That night, though, Sam and I both shouted out, 'What's the time? Our watches have stopped.'

'So that's your excuse, is it?' said Sean. He looked down at his watch. I was dead certain he was going to say it was half past twelve or something. Instead he said, 'It's just gone quarter past nine.' Sam and I looked at each other in amazement.

'So there's no missing time,' whispered Sam.

'No,' I whispered back. Of course I was relieved but I was just a tiny bit disappointed too.

'You'll have to think of a better excuse than that,' said Sean. 'I don't think Auntie Judy's going to believe both your watches stopped at the same time.'

'But it's the truth,' I said. 'We saw a spaceship and it set my beeper off and stopped both our watches.'

'Spaceship!' exclaimed Sean. 'Tell me, are you two being looked after by nurses?'

'Honestly, we have just seen one!' cried Sam. 'It was here, right on the common!'

'Of course it was,' said Sean, laughing.

'Look, it really happened!' I said this so dramatically that the smile froze on Sean's face.

'We thought it was a very bright star at first,' I continued, 'but then it got nearer and nearer to us. And I saw these aliens inside; I could see one of them really clearly.'

'What did they look like then?' asked Sean. He was grinning again now.

'Well, they were completely bald,' I began.

'Probably thought you were their long-lost cousin,' interrupted Sean. Then he stopped suddenly, afraid he'd been too rude. But I'm always the first to see the joke. (If people see you getting narked then they'll never stop.)

'They also had dark, wraparound eyes and tiny slits for a mouth,' I said.

'Exactly like your mask in fact,' said Sean, drily. 'Amazing. Have you got anything to add to this, Sam?'

'Well, I never actually saw any aliens,' she said.

'Shame.' Sean shook his head.

'But I did see everything else Freddie described, and the spaceship really did seem to be making straight for us.'

'OK. I'll tell you exactly what you saw,' explained Sean. 'You saw someone in a huge aeroplane or helicopter.'

'No,' we chorused together.

'All right, it was a meteor . . .'

'A meteor couldn't stop in the air,' I interrupted. 'And how about both our watches stopping at exactly the same moment, and . . .' I undid a couple of buttons on my shirt, 'feel this.'

'I'd rather not.'

'No, go on.'

Sean extended an unwilling hand. 'All right, you're sweating like a pig. But that's not proof.'

'Isn't it?' interrupted Sam.

Sean continued, 'What I want to know is, if little green men are dropping in on us every four seconds, why don't they ever leave us any proof? Why can't they say, "Here's a pebble from the planet Mercury", or, "Do have a jar full of our unique, blue sand" . . . but they never ever do that, do they? Why not?'

'Well . . .' I hesitated.

'Because they only exist in people's imaginations.'

'You can't say that,' I replied.

'Yes I can, because there's a rational explanation for every spooky happening. You've just got to look for it. Like a mate of mine was out late one night when he saw this ghostly figure whirling about in the distance. It just came out of nowhere, and his first impulse was to run for his life. But instead he decided to investigate, so he carried on walking

towards it. And in the end he worked out what it was: a fire on the horizon that had caught the light. Yet, for a few crazy seconds he really thought he'd seen a face in that flame . . . a ghost. But like I said, there's always a proper reason.' He lowered his voice. 'Still, do you get the curious feeling we're not quite alone here?'

'Yes,' I whispered.

'Well, we're not.' Then grinning, Sean pointed to Miss West who was walking briskly towards us.

I groaned loudly. 'What's she doing here? I bet she's going to give us a lecture.' But instead she was contorting her face into what seemed in this dim light like a smile.

'Greetings everyone. My meeting finished earlier than I expected, so I thought I'd come and see how you are, Sam.'

'She's been UFO-spotting,' scoffed Sean.

'But how fascinating,' replied Miss West. 'Such sightings are a special interest of mine. You must tell me exactly what happened.'

And we did. Only Miss West never once looked in my direction. Sam had all her attention. Afterwards Sean said, 'I told them there's a perfectly rational explanation for all this.'

'Well, I'm sure there's an explanation,' replied Miss West. 'Now would you two boys mind leaving us alone for a moment. I want to have a word with Sam.'

Don't ask me why, but I wasn't too keen on leaving Sam on her own with Miss West. However Sean practically pulled me away.

When we got home Auntie Judy was in no mood to discuss UFOs. She gave me this really stern lecture about how I must always tell her where I was going. After a cup of hot chocolate I was sent up to bed. There was still no sign of Sam, or Miss West.

Sean popped his head in. 'Your watch hasn't stopped again, has it? Because you know what that means: either you're about to hitch a ride with E.T.

or you need new batteries.' Then he said, quite seriously, 'I'd just forget the whole thing if I were you.'

'I can't do that.'

'Well, look on it as a bad dream.' He climbed up to his room – the deluxe room I call it – in the attic.

Then I heard Sam come back. I'd been listening out for her. Auntie Judy was saying something to Sam and Miss West for a while. Auntie Judy didn't sound very happy at all.

At last Sam trundled up the stairs. I met her on the landing.

'So, what did Miss West want?'

'To tell me she's all packed and ready to move to Brighton, the day after tomorrow.'

'Excellent.'

'And to ask me if I wanted to come away for a few days with her.'

'What did you say?'

'No, of course.'

I grinned at her. 'How do you feel?'

'Strange.'

'So what's new?'

She smiled. 'The tips of my fingers are still tingling. And I still feel a bit . . . scared. Do you?'

'Oh no,' I said airily, but really I did.

'What we saw tonight on the common,' she said,

'I don't think we should go on about it so much.'

I looked puzzled.

'I think Sean's right,' she went on. 'There probably is an explanation. There's got to be.'

'Yeah, the explanation is, we saw an alien spaceship.'

'No, no.' She shook her head. 'We just got ourselves all worked up. We started believing all sorts of things. I mean, we thought there was some missing time, but there wasn't, was there?'

'No,' I conceded.

'So what we saw was something, but it wasn't an alien spaceship.'

'Even though I saw aliens sitting inside it.'

'Look, I know you want to see aliens and tonight you thought you did. But I don't, all right.' Her voice had gone all high and squeaky.

I stared at her indignantly. 'It sounds like you're blaming me for what we saw.'

'Don't be silly.'

'You are, aren't you?'

'Yes I am,' she cried. 'All the time you go on about aliens and abductions and missing time. No wonder we start imagining . . .'

'We didn't imagine anything.'

'Freddie!' She was practically shrieking at me now. 'How do you think I'm going to sleep tonight?'

'So I'm giving you nightmares now, am I?'

'Yes you are, because you just can't stop talking about aliens. You care more about them than you do about real people.' Sam stopped abruptly, as if realizing she'd said more than she'd intended.

'You can't say that,' I hissed.

'I just have,' she replied.

We glared at each other.

Auntie Judy called up the stairs. 'Right, into your own rooms now. It's a school day tomorrow.' Without another word we marched into our rooms. I slammed the door shut. Then, like an echo, Sam slammed her door shut a second later.

I prowled around my room unable to settle. I couldn't keep still. How could Sam say I cared more about aliens than humans, than her?

I stared at my aliens all lined up on the shelf. I used to pretend I was their ruler and this was my own private universe. I still do, sometimes. But there's nothing wrong with that, is there?

I picked up the mask. This afternoon when I'd been the alien had been the greatest moment of my life. Afterwards came this great storm of cheering and whistling for me. I just lapped it up. But now it was ruined. Now this mask looked cheap and pathetic; it was just like something from a joke shop.

And so was I.

Finally, I couldn't bear to look at the mask any more. So I chucked it in the bin.

Then I got into bed. 'The mask's gone now . . . Pleasant dreams, Sam,' I hissed.

## CHAPTER SEVEN
### *by Sam*

That night I pulled the covers right up to my head. But later, I felt something pulling the covers away from me. I opened my eyes. I let out a cry. I wasn't in my bedroom any more. I was back at the scene of my accident. Only this time I was sitting up.

Something stirred in front of me. I saw a shadow wavering about. Then a shape began to form — a shape wearing a grey suit and a wide-brimmed hat.

He began to look at me.

I knew I should look away.

I knew I was in danger.

'Was it you on the spaceship?' I cried. 'Was it?' He didn't answer.

But his eyes held me. Terrible, unearthly eyes which seemed to bore right through me. Then all at once I was on my feet and moving towards him. My feet didn't even touch the floor. I felt oddly weightless.

He was beckoning to me. I didn't want to go any nearer. But I couldn't stop myself.

To my horror I went floating right up to him . . .

## CHAPTER EIGHT
### by Freddie

I couldn't get to sleep. So I lay in bed looking at my 3D stars. They glow in the dark. But you've got to keep recharging them by 'exposing them to a light bulb'. That's what it says on the packet. And it always makes me laugh.

I needed some laughs that night. Normally my bedroom was the only place where I felt safe. But tonight, the fear had even crept in here.

I couldn't stop thinking about that spaceship – and those aliens looking out at me. What did it mean? Would the aliens strike again? I was scared. That's why I had to keep talking about it. Sam didn't understand that. I was still angry with her . . . with everyone.

Normally my dad's photograph lived on the bedside table beside me. It was of my dad a few years ago now, and it was in black and white. But it was a good picture of him. He was looking straight into the camera and smiling as if nothing in the world could ever bother him.

I used to think my dad's photo watched over me while I was asleep. Now I've turned the photo over just as if it's in disgrace.

I closed my eyes. I could hear the house creaking and shuddering. All houses do that and I wish they wouldn't. Then I heard a new sound: a door opening downstairs.

I sat straight up in bed. Aliens had got into the house and they were searching for me. But then I heard what sounded like a cupboard click open. I couldn't imagine aliens wanting to rifle through our cupboards.

But someone else did. Who?

Uncle Tony sometimes got up to make a cup of tea in the night. But he was away. I'd never known Auntie Judy go downstairs. She slept like a top. So did Sean.

I knocked twice on the wall to Sam. She didn't answer. She must be asleep. Or maybe she was just pretending.

From downstairs came the sound of another cupboard opening. It had to be a burglar. Well, I was going to deal with this by myself. That would show Sam. I scrambled out of bed, flung on my dressing-gown, then I reached out for my mask, forgetting I'd thrown it away. I rescued the mask from the bin and put it on again. I figured it might give the burglar a bit of a shock, and anyway, I felt braver behind it.

For good measure I took my ray-gun as well. It was supposed to fire poison darts which caused your victim to disintegrate little by little (on the box it promised your victim would leave a trail of black furry dust). Sadly, it did nothing of the sort. Still, the burglar might not know that.

Armed, I advanced down the stairs. Then I stopped. Someone was clinking keys about now.

Brandishing my ray-gun I charged forward. 'Don't move, or I'll punch your lights out!'

But I was talking to the air. The kitchen door swung open, the key still in the lock. I rushed outside. I immediately spotted Sam in her nightdress. She was pulling open the back gate and walking past the side of our house. Where was she going? 'Sam. Sam.'

She stopped. She looked back at me.

'Sam, what are you doing out here?'

She turned round. 'You called me,' she said.

'I called you. What are you gabbling on about? Look, it's the middle of the night, get back inside.'

She slowly moved towards me. Something else moved too. A tall shadow disturbed the darkness. It stirred as if turning its head to watch Sam and me. Did I see the outline of a hat? I wasn't sure. And it didn't move again. It just seemed to vanish away. All my courage vanished with it. 'Hurry up,' I whispered to Sam.

She didn't have her arms outstretched like sleepwalkers do in films, but she followed me in a slow, trance-like way back to the kitchen. I put the ray-gun on the table. She was hovering uncertainly in the doorway, as if she'd never been in there before.

'Well, come on, sit down,' I said. She was kind of spooky, to be honest. Especially her eyes, which had this really odd, glazed expression. But she obeyed me, sitting bolt upright on one of the kitchen chairs.

'Sam, can you understand what I'm saying?'

'Yes, I can understand what you're saying.'

She could hear me all right, so she was partly awake. And yet, she was also asleep. Her voice was dull and expressionless, not like her normal voice at all. It was as if she'd been hypnotized. I wanted to shake her awake. But you're not supposed to ever do that to a sleep-walker, are you?

She was staring at me as if awaiting her next instruction. So, on impulse, I cried out, 'Get up and touch your toes.'

At once she did just that.

'Do it four more times,' I ordered. Again she obeyed, counting aloud as she did so.

Suddenly she was completely in my power. If I told her to rob a bank she'd go off and do it. Not that I would ever ask her to do that. But then I had this really silly idea. Just as a joke I said, 'Repeat this after me.' I could hardly speak for laughing. 'I really fancy Freddie Burden.'

Sam just looked puzzled.

She'd probably understand me better if I wasn't wearing this mask. It was getting really hot anyhow. I whipped the mask off.

'Now, repeat after me . . .'

But a new light had suddenly appeared in Sam's eyes. She was gazing all around her in bewilderment. 'Freddie, what . . . what's happening?'

'It's OK. Don't panic. You've just been doing a spot of sleep-walking.'

She jolted with shock. 'Where did I go?'

'You were going out of the back gate when I stopped you.'

'What?' She gazed down at the soles of her feet which were splattered with mud. She looked back at me again. 'So if you hadn't brought me back inside I could have ended up anywhere.'

'That's right. I didn't wake you up because they say if you wake up a sleep-walker both their legs fall off or something.'

But she didn't smile. Instead, she shivered. 'Oh Freddie, this is terrible. And I had the same dream, you know.'

I started at that. 'You did?'

'Yes.' She shook her head miserably. 'I was there at the accident again and so was he. Only today he was commanding me with his eyes. I couldn't refuse.' Her voice shook. 'It was as if he'd put me under a spell.'

I leaned forward and squeezed her hand. 'Hey, come on. Look, I'll make you a cup of tea.' This is what Auntie Judy always did when anyone was upset. I filled the kettle with water and switched it on. Then I busied about making the tea.

'There, get that down your choppers,' I said, banging a mug down in front of her.

She began to drink. Normally she moans about my tea (I make good tea but it's really strong), but that night she just gulped it right down.

'I've never slept-walked before you know,' she said.

'Oh, I have, heaps of times. Once I got up and put my pillow down the toilet.'

'Why?'

'Haven't a clue.'

'Only you could do that, Freddie.' She smiled at

me. 'Still, if it hadn't been for you I dread to think where I'd be now. I'm very grateful.'

Now that's something I don't often hear. I felt brave and noble. And I couldn't help digging about for a bit more gratitude.

'Sam, when you were outside tonight, I think someone else was out there too.' She didn't reply – she was too busy choking. I should have stopped there. But I didn't. 'I saw this shadow move, I couldn't see the face at all, but I think I made out a large hat. Still, when he saw me . . .' I stopped, awaiting a fresh supply of gratitude. It never arrived.

A look of horror seemed to be stuck on her face. 'So you think someone was waiting outside for me . . . someone wearing a large hat.' She was speaking very slowly.

'I couldn't be completely certain about the hat.' I gave a nervous laugh. Something was wrong here.

'But how would he know I was going to sleep-walk and go outside?'

'Well, maybe – and this is just an idea – the man you saw at the accident is an alien, who is control-ling you through your dreams.' I stopped. I could see this theory wasn't going down very well. 'Of course the shadow might just have been a stranger who happened to be passing. After all, lots of people wear hats, don't they?'

It was too late.

'You're doing it again, aren't you?' cried Sam.

'What?'

'You're really scaring me.'

'Oh come on,' I cried indignantly. 'If it hadn't been for me . . .'

'I might not even have gone sleep-walking,' she interrupted.

'Excuse me, but you're the one who saw the nightmare man.'

'Not outside my house.'

'Look, I didn't say it was definitely him.'

'Yes you did.'

'No, I said someone was hanging about – and he looked like he was wearing a hat.'

'I don't want to hear!' she screamed, putting her hands over her ears.

'Now, you're being really pathetic,' I said.

'Just go away. I don't ever want to talk to you again.'

'What's going on here?' Auntie Judy's voice made us both jump.

'Sam's been sleep-walking,' I said. 'I stopped her.' I gave Sam a look.

'And Freddie says he saw someone outside. An alien,' said Sam.

'I never said he was an alien,' I snapped.

'Stop all this,' cried Auntie Judy. 'Do you want to wake Sean as well? Now, first I suggest we all just lower the temperature, all right.' This was one of Auntie Judy's favourite expressions when she wanted us to calm down.

Sam sat there with her arms folded, breathing really fast. Another time I might have felt sorry for her. Tonight all I could think about was how deeply ungrateful she was. I was only telling her what happened. And someone *had* been out there.

But soon Auntie Judy was having a go at me as well. 'I think it's best we forget all this, don't you, Freddie? You probably just saw a cat.'

'A pretty big cat,' I muttered. 'A giant cat, in fact.'

Auntie Judy glanced at my ray-gun and alien mask on the kitchen table. 'And I think it's time we stopped all this talk of aliens and UFOs, Freddie. Sam had a nasty fall recently and she's still not quite herself.'

I didn't trust myself to reply.

Sam went back to bed first.

I followed. I stood outside her door and hissed, 'Blame me for tonight if it makes you feel any better – until you find the real culprit.'

She didn't answer.

I'd just recharged my stars once more when I thought I heard the phone click in Auntie Judy's room.

Then I decided that was impossible. After all, who would Auntie Judy be calling at half past two in the morning?

# CHAPTER NINE
## *by Sam*

Next morning Freddie and I walked to school in silence.

I wished I hadn't said some of the things I had to Freddie last night. He'd been a good friend to me, and helped me a lot, especially when I first came here.

But I was still annoyed with him too. I went cold right to my bones when he said someone was waiting outside the house for me last night. An alien, too, he reckoned. Why did he have to be so hypey about everything? Sean was right: there must be a rational explanation for all these strange events. We should be looking for that, not scaring each other all the time.

I knew Freddie was cross with me too. I hated this bad atmosphere. I wanted to make up. But we didn't.

Just as we got to school I said, 'Freddie, I'd rather you didn't tell anyone about what we thought we saw on the common – or me sleep-walking.'

Normally when he talks to you Freddie's eyes are springing about all over the place. Today they were blank and still. 'My lips are sealed,' he said flatly. It was strange seeing Freddie without even the trace of a smile on his face. Again, I wanted to make up. And again the words stuck in my throat.

The day passed slowly. My eyes burned with tiredness. My aunt didn't tell the class she was leaving until right at the end of the day. There were muffled cheers. No-one could hide their delight.

'Let me ask how you think you have benefited from my classes?'

There was a long, terrible silence. Finally I had to say something, just out of family loyalty. 'I think we work more quietly now,' I said.

'Yes, you're calmer than you were before.' She always spoke to the class as if it were one person. 'I think you've benefited from my training, in so many ways.'

There were half-hearted murmurs in agreement. I wondered if Aunt Margaret knew everyone was just humouring her.

Even though it was her last lesson, she insisted we file out in silence. Outside, though, there were loud cheers. I almost felt sorry for my aunt having to hear that. But she didn't seem bothered.

'Well, I'm off to get some sea air now. You can still come for a few days, you know, Sam. There's plenty of room where I'm staying, and your head-mistress is agreeable to you having this time away.'

I felt mean. But my home was with Uncle Tony and Auntie Judy, Sean and Freddie, especially now when I was feeling so confused. I tried to explain this to Aunt Margaret.

'I wish you'd trust me,' she interrupted, twisting her thin lips into a smile.

My face reddened.

'You really do need this time away – with me.' She gave me one of her piercing stares. I had to look away.

'I'm sorry, I can't,' I murmured.

'I see.' Her smile had gone. Her eyebrows hovered menacingly. 'You don't make things easy for yourself, do you?'

I thought that was an odd thing to say. Before I could reply she'd picked up her bag and walked out.

I walked over to the lockers. That's where Freddie and I wait for each other. I wasn't sure if he'd be there today. But he was.

'Your aunt looked happy,' said Freddie.

'She was cross I wouldn't go away with her.'

'I'd rather go away with Godzilla.'

I smiled, then looked away. 'Thanks for waiting.'

'I nearly didn't.'

'You know I didn't mean what I said last night about . . .'

'About me preferring aliens to people. That's a terrible thing to say to anyone.' He sounded like a teacher telling me off.

'Yes, all right, but I was really upset last night – and when you're upset you say things, stupid things, don't you?'

'You made me feel a right plum.'

I looked up. 'Oh, come on Freddie, you know you're my best friend.'

I thought he was going to say something similar back to me. Instead, he grabbed my bag and ran all the way to the school gates with it.

'Wait, you know I can't run fast at the moment,' I wailed.

At the gates he did turn round and wait, then with a little bow he handed my bag back to me. 'Let's go home,' he said.

We walked out of school together.

'Just one thing, Freddie. Can we please not talk about aliens any more.'

'No problem. I can talk about other things you know.'

'Can you really,' I replied, in mock surprise.

'OK, here's something to think about. If Dracula's got no reflection, how come he's always got such a straight parting?'

I started to laugh and Freddie was grinning all over his face now. (If you want to get on with Freddie, just laugh at one of his silly jokes. You'll be his friend for life.)

Suddenly, I noticed I hadn't shut my bag properly. I was about to close it when I got a shock. A book I'd never seen before was sitting right on the top. I picked it up very cautiously. Its title was in bold red letters: ALIEN ENCOUNTERS.

An icy fear raced down my body. 'Freddie, did you put this in my bag?'

'What?' He glanced at the title. 'No, I did not,

and don't you start blaming me . . .'

'I'm not.' The book shook in my hand.

'It's no big deal. Someone probably just put it in your bag for a joke.'

'But no-one knows about the UFO.' I looked at him. 'Do they?'

'I promised you I wouldn't tell anyone and I haven't.' Freddie took the book from me and inspected it. 'It's from the school library . . . still got the ticket inside too.'

'So someone's nicked it and planted it on me. I'd better take it back.'

'You sure you didn't take it by accident?'

I gave Freddie a stare.

'All right, just testing. Do you want me to take it back tomorrow?'

'No, I'll do it now.'

'Well, I'll come with you.'

But then Freddie discovered he'd left his Arsenal scarf behind in the classroom. I couldn't wait for him. I wanted to get rid of the book right now.

If it had been a book about anything else it wouldn't have unnerved me so much. But someone had passed on a book about aliens to me. Was it just a very eerie coincidence?

I rushed inside the library. Mrs Ibbot, the librarian, always opened it for half an hour after school. Often it would get quite busy.

But today there was no sign of Mrs Ibbot, or anyone else. It was deathly still. Even the blinds were all drawn. Then I remembered Mrs Ibbot was away on a course; the library had been closed all day.

I would just leave the book on the desk. But at that moment the book seemed to come alive; it slipped from my grasp and dived on to the carpet. I jumped back in alarm. Out of its pages sprung a small card. I knelt down and looked at the card. Then I picked it up.

In large black capitals was written one word:

GLABULA. What did it mean? Maybe nothing? Or maybe it was a word in a foreign language? Still, what did it matter? The card didn't belong to me. Yet, somehow I sensed I was meant to see that card.

I glanced around me nervously. All I could hear was my unsteady breathing. I was getting out of here, fast. I picked the book up, flung it down onto the desk, then made for the door.

I never reached it. A cracking sound, like wood snapping stopped me dead in my tracks. Behind me came a sudden burst of light. A blind must have gone flying up into the air. And all at once I had the STRANGEST feeling I wasn't alone. I was being watched. I couldn't see who it was because my neck wouldn't turn round. Neither would my head.

Then, finally, I managed one quick glance. That glance was enough to make my heart freeze with horror. He was out there, staring in through the window at me.

'Freddie!' I yelled. 'He's jumped out of my night-mare. He's here!' But there was no answering call from Freddie.

I slowly turned round, half expecting the man to vanish away like a bad dream. But he didn't. He stood there in his usual grey suit and wide-brimmed, black hat, not moving a muscle.

'Who are you?' I cried. 'What do you want?'

He didn't answer, but slowly stretched a hand towards me as if beckoning me forward. Only it didn't look like a human's hand, as he only had three large fingers.

Weren't aliens supposed to only have three fingers? Hadn't Freddie told me that? This man was an alien who'd somehow got right inside my head, even into my dreams.

He stretched his hand out again, then let it fall slowly and deliberately onto his shoulder as if he were making some kind of sign.

A trembling ran right through me. I had to get away. I ran to the door. But I couldn't open it. Someone must have locked the door. But that was impossible. In a panic I pulled and pulled at it. Suddenly from behind me came a great rush of air. I whirled round. I couldn't believe what I saw. I stood there, gaping with horror.

Somehow he'd got inside the library. And now he was slowly walking towards me, still with one arm outstretched.

'Get away from me!' I cried, backing against the door. He didn't answer, just carried on walking towards me. I pounded on that door and screamed Freddie's name. Then, to my great relief, I heard footsteps. I yelled out, 'Help! Help!' Moments later I could see Freddie's anxious face staring in at me. 'The door's locked. I can't get out and . . .'

Freddie turned the handle. At once the door sprang open and I practically fell on to him.

'He's here, Freddie! He's in the library!'

Freddie looked at me for a moment. 'Right,' he whispered, then marched inside the library. I went after him. He patrolled around the whole room, even though it was quite obvious the library was empty once more.

Freddie went over and looked out of the window. 'No sign of anyone — except the old caretaker pottering about,' he announced.

'But he was in here,' I cried. 'You do believe me?'

'Of course I do.' He sounded indignant. He pulled out a chair. 'And you'd better sit down before you fall down.'

I sank onto that chair. I put my head between my knees. My heart was still pounding away. I began to recover my breath. I looked up. Freddie was staring intently at me.

'Feel any better?' he asked.

'A bit.'

'So what exactly happened?'

I told him everything. Then I asked, 'But you never saw . . . ?'

'Your nightmare man?'

'Oh, don't call him my nightmare man, please.'

'OK, sorry. But no, I didn't see him.'

'He was here though.'

'I believe you. And you can't blame me this time.'

'I know. Where have you been, anyway?'

'Well, I was in the classroom getting my scarf when your aunt popped up and started chatting to me . . . I've never known her to be so chummy. It was hard to get away from her.' He stopped. 'Maybe she was keeping me away from here deliberately.'

'What?'

'She could be in league with him.'

'No,' I began.

'Just a suggestion. Did you get a close look at him?'

'He was dressed exactly as before. He had the same huge dark eyes and, oh yes, he only had three fingers.'

Freddie leaned forward.

'That means he's an alien, doesn't it?' I asked.

'Aliens do often have three fingers. How did you know that?' asked Freddie.

'You must have told me. So he really is one.' I paused and closed my eyes for a moment. 'But why's he after me?' I half-whispered.

'Obviously an alien with very poor taste.'

I managed a small smile.

'Well, you are a bit of a brain-box,' went on Freddie, 'just right for them to do tests on. You're probably their prize target. I reckon he's trying to hypnotize you by giving you all these dreams . . .'

'So that one day I will follow him.' I shuddered. 'And it was as if he knew I'd be in the library. Do you think he planted that book on me?'

'Or someone working with him did – which brings us back to your aunt. Sometimes aliens join forces with a humanoid – and I'm not saying that to scare you,' he added hastily.

Then Freddie spotted the card. He picked it up.

'Oh yes, that flew out of the book. It just has one word on it: GLABULA.'

'Where?' He sounded puzzled.

Freddie handed me the card. I caught my breath. It was blank.

'But there *was* something on there: GLABULA in big capitals. I saw it.'

'Glabula,' repeated Freddie. 'Never heard of it.'

'Nor have I. And I've got a smattering of French and German.'

'You can get a cream for that.'

'No, this isn't funny. I see a strange word on a card, then the word vanishes. Freddie, am I going nutty?'

He shrugged his shoulders. 'I couldn't tell you, but then I've been nutty for years.'

'Last night I really wanted it to be you the aliens were targeting, then I tried to persuade myself it was all just imagination – but it's not, is it? Something is after me, and there's more to come, isn't there?'

'Listen,' whispered Freddie urgently. Someone was coming down the corridor. We both got to our feet, sensing danger.

Miss West opened the door. 'Sam, what are you doing in here?'

'I came to put a book back, and I saw someone.'

'Who?'

'It was the man I saw at the accident and in my

nightmares. He was watching me and then he was inside the library and . . .'

'This nonsense has gone on long enough. You must let me help you. You will come to Brighton with me for a few days. You need some time away from here to help clear your head.'

'No, I don't,' I began.

'I'm afraid I'm going to insist now, Sam,' continued Aunt Margaret.

'You can't do that,' Freddie and I chorused.

'I think you'll find I can,' she said, pursing her lips. 'I am, after all, your only relative and I am very concerned about you.'

'But I'm fine really,' I cried.

'Clearly you're not. But after a few days with me, you will be cured. I can promise you that.'

She really emphasized the word 'cured' making it sound as if I was very ill.

She was starting to unnerve me.

'Trust me, Sam,' she said, stretching out a hand to me, then her hand slowly fell onto her shoulder. Just a few moments ago the nightmare man had made exactly the same gesture.

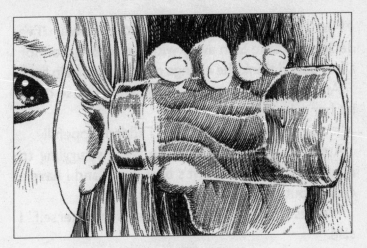

## CHAPTER TEN
### by Freddie

So then Miss West drove Sam and me home. And she was still saying how Sam had to go away with her. I thought my head was going to explode – with anger.

I snapped. 'You can't just abduct people away, you know. It's against the law.'

Miss West didn't answer, but her chin jutted forward determinedly. Sam sat next to me in the back of the car. She didn't say anything either, just looked sick.

Auntie Judy walked out of the house to meet us. She knew at once something was wrong.

Miss West wound the window down. 'I've decided to take Sam away with me to Brighton for a few days. I think the change of scene will help her.'

'And I don't want to go,' cried Sam. 'Please don't let her take me away.'

'It's against the law, isn't it?' I added, hopefully.

Auntie Judy looked as if she were struggling to control herself. 'I think it's best if you and I have a chat about this,' she said to Miss West.

'It's best if Sam's allowed to decide for herself,' I said.

Miss West got out of the car, rather reluctantly I thought. Auntie Judy turned to Sam and me. 'Don't worry, this will all be sorted out soon. Why don't you two chill out in the den.'

Sam and I went to the den but we didn't stay there long.

'I bet they're in the lounge,' I said. 'Let's go and listen.'

Sam hesitated. 'Isn't that a bit tacky?'

I gave her a look. 'Don't be daft. If people are talking about you behind your back you've got every right to listen. I've always done it . . . and after all, it's your life that's being decided behind that door.'

'You're quite right,' she said.

'Of course I am.'

So we went and pinned our ears right against the lounge door. Auntie Judy and Miss West were definitely in there. You could make out the odd word, but that was all, because they were both talking so quietly.

'I feel like going in there and asking them to speak up,' said Sam.

'I could accidentally push the door open,' I replied.

'No, no.'

Then I remembered an old trick, used it lots of times. I grabbed a glass and put the stem against the door. I tried to steady it. It scraped down the door. I thought Auntie Judy and Miss West might have heard it and stopped talking, but they didn't seem to notice, perhaps because they were arguing so intently.

I could pick up a few words now. I repeated them to Sam.

'Miss West is saying it's the only way,' I hissed.

Sam's face fell. 'But now Auntie Judy's having a go. She said, "All you're doing is bullying the girl".'

'That's telling her,' said Sam.

'Miss West is spouting again, but she's whispering so faintly . . .'

'That means she's really mad,' murmured Sam.

'Now they seem to have stopped . . . I think they're coming out.'

We sprinted back to the den, just as the lounge door opened.

More doors slammed, then there was silence.

'What's happening now?' asked Sam.

I shrugged my shoulders.

'Freddie, what will I do if Aunt Margaret has won?' The blood seemed to have drained out of her cheeks. She was deathly pale.

I replied, as confidently as I could, 'Don't worry, we'll run away somewhere, do something.' Then came quick footsteps.

It was Auntie Judy. She looked tense but she was speaking in that reassuring voice she keeps for moments like this.

'Sam, your Aunt Margaret and I had a good discussion and we both feel that this isn't the right time for you to go away.'

I let out a huge sigh of relief, then asked, 'Has she slung her hook then?'

'Miss West's leaving for Brighton tomorrow as planned, if that's what you mean, Freddie,' replied Auntie Judy. 'But she's looking forward to seeing Sam very soon.'

'Not if Sam sees her first,' I muttered.

'But I haven't got to go,' exclaimed Sam.

'Oh, love, of course not,' replied Auntie Judy. 'You haven't got to go until you're ready.'

'That'll be never then,' said Sam. Then she gave Auntie Judy an enormous hug.

I felt a bit left out until Sam smiled across at me. Her eyes had gone all shiny. I expect mine were a bit shiny too.

Then Sam told Auntie Judy what had happened in the library. Auntie Judy immediately asked, 'Freddie, where were you when this was going on?'

'Stuck in a classroom with Miss West. So you can't blame me.' I added, 'I do not have control over aliens. I only look like one.'

Auntie Judy patted my shoulder. 'I just want to

give Sam a chance to heal naturally. And to do that she will need to forget all about UFOs and aliens for a while and think about other things like . . .'

'Like nice little fairies and elves, you mean,' I said.

Auntie Judy smiled. 'I just want you two to stop scaring each other.'

When Auntie Judy left to answer the phone Sam hissed, 'Freddie, there's something I haven't told you about the man in the library.'

'It's not going to scare me, is it? Because from now on I only want to talk about dear little pixies . . .' But Sam wasn't laughing, so I said instead, 'Come on then, spill it.'

'The nightmare man. When he was talking to me he raised his hand, then let it fall onto his opposite shoulder.'

'Bit weird, I suppose.'

'Then, when we were in the library Aunt Margaret made exactly the same gesture.'

'Did she?'

Sam nodded vigorously. 'Strange coincidence – or what?'

'Or what?' I said softly. 'I think when your aunt goes to Brighton these spooky things will stop. The alien – or whatever he is – will have lost his main accomplice.'

Sam frowned. 'I know my aunt's dead strange but I just can't believe she would really hand me over to aliens.'

'Well, she knew you'd come back unharmed, except for the odd scar and some tinfoil up your nose.' I leaned forward. 'Of course we've got no proof she truly is your aunt. For all we know she might have disposed of your real aunt – after all, you hadn't met her before – and taken her place.'

Sam was grinning. 'And why would she do that?'

'Because you've come into some money and she wants to get her hands on it. So she turns up with her accomplice, gives you bad dreams, and tries to scare you.'

'So then everyone will think I'm mad and she'll get all my money.'

'It's a clever scheme, isn't it?'

'Amazing.'

Then we both burst out laughing. We were still laughing when Auntie Judy appeared. 'This is what I like to see, you two relaxing.'

That set us both giggling again until I saw Auntie Judy waving a letter around. 'I'm very sorry, Freddie, I should have given you this before. It arrived second post today.'

I grabbed the letter. I held it tight. I felt excited, and sick together.

I knew at once who it was from.

## CHAPTER ELEVEN
### *by Sam*

That evening I only set two places for tea. Sean had gone to a party and would be sleeping over – and Freddie wasn't hungry. He hadn't come downstairs since getting his letter.

I quizzed Auntie Judy over the meal about it. 'Was the letter from Freddie's dad?'

Auntie Judy nodded slowly.

'Was it bad news?'

'I'm sure Freddie will want to tell you about it himself.'

I couldn't help fishing a bit more. 'Did his dad explain why he missed the meal?'

Auntie Judy nodded slowly again.

'And do you know why?'

'I think I do.'

But that was all Auntie Judy would say. She never gossiped. I asked her something about Sean's family once and straightaway this great wall of silence went up around her. It was there again now.

Auntie Judy changed the subject. 'Uncle Tony rang. His flight from Germany is due at Heathrow, five o'clock tomorrow.'

'I bet you're looking forward to that.'

Her cheeks turned pink. 'Yes I am.'

'Does he speak German?' I asked.

'Fluently. He's quite a good linguist, actually.'

'Perhaps he'll know the meaning of this word I saw today, then.'

'What's that?'

'Funny word, I'm not sure how you pronounce it: *Glabula*.'

Auntie Judy looked away from me. Her voice

tightened. 'Where did you come across that word?'

'It was really weird. You know I found this book about aliens in my bag. I forgot to tell you, this card flew out of the book, with just this one word written on it: *Glabula*. Do you know what it means?'

For a second anger flashed into Auntie Judy's eyes. 'No, I don't know that word, I'd just forget it if I were you.' Then she gave me such an odd smile. Suddenly, Auntie Judy didn't look like herself.

I was just being daft now. Yet since the accident people have acted so oddly. Aunt Margaret has certainly been peculiar, changing into someone I don't know or trust. And now even my beloved Auntie Judy was beginning to feel like a stranger sometimes, as well.

There was only Freddie left. Straight after I'd helped wash up I raced upstairs. I went into my bedroom and knocked twice on the wall. To my relief Freddie immediately gave two knocks in reply.

He was sitting on his bed, swinging that alien mask around in his hand. 'Thought you'd been abducted,' he said.

'Auntie Judy said you wanted to be on your own.'

'No, I just wasn't hungry.'

'She said your dad wrote to you.'

He picked up the letter. 'Yeah, he did . . . you're more than welcome to read it.'

'Oh, right, thanks.'

'He's got neater handwriting than me – and doesn't make so many spelling mistakes.'

I began reading. It was a strange letter – very polite and oddly formal, more like a letter from a distant relative than from a dad. He started off by apologizing for cancelling the meal at the last minute. He said he'd wanted to see Freddie so much but just before he set off he'd lost his courage. He wanted to tell Freddie his secret but he couldn't do it face to face.

He went on to explain that over the past years he had not been abroad on business as Freddie had supposed. He had got friends to post the cards to Freddie for him. Instead, he had done 'something very foolish' five years ago to try and make some easy money – and as a result had spent these past years in prison.

I looked up. Freddie was staring at me very closely as if watching for my reaction. I wasn't sure how to react. I gave him a brief smile, then read on.

Freddie's dad wrote that the years in prison had been the worst in his life. He had hated it there. But it did give him time to 'review his life' and gain some qualifications. He listed all the exams he'd passed, just as if he were applying for a job. He said he was determined to work hard and make good now.

He was very sorry he'd had to lie to Freddie – but he'd only done that to protect him. He hoped Freddie would understand that.

One day he wanted Freddie to come and live with him so that they could make a real home together. But that decision would always be Freddie's (this was underlined).

He would ring Freddie very soon. If Freddie would talk to him that would mean more than anything. He signed it: *With kind regards, from your dad*.

I stopped reading. Freddie flung the alien mask up into the air and caught it. Then he said, 'So that's the kind of dad I've got . . . a convict.'

'I won't tell anyone,' I burst out, and immediately wished I hadn't said that.

'I always suspected there was something funny about him,' said Freddie. 'The way he could never find the time to see me . . . I mean, no-one's that busy.'

'He said he was trying to protect you.'

'Yeah, well it's nothing to do with me. I mean, it's his fault if he breaks the law. No-one else's.'

I desperately tried to think what else to say. I didn't want to say the wrong thing. 'It's good he wants to contact you though.'

'Is it?'

'He'll take you out for that meal properly next time.'

'Will you come?'

The question took me by surprise. 'Yes, of course I will.'

'Well, don't get too excited, he probably won't turn up again.'

'I think he will,' I said, quietly.

'Do you?'

'Yes, I do.'

He looked at me as if wanting me to say more. Struggling now, I said, 'I suppose . . . I suppose it must be a bit strange for him returning, after being away for all those years.'

'He's been in prison, not on Mars.'

'I know, but perhaps he rushed it a bit before. Now he's really ready to see you.'

Freddie looked around him. 'I know we're not a normal family here but we get on all right, don't we? I'm not very hard done-by.' He clenched his hands. 'I don't need him.' He turned away.

'You could just talk to him.'

'I don't think so.' He turned round again. 'Maybe Miss West will post you a note tonight telling you her deep, dark secrets. I bet she's got loads. You should be safe tonight . . . but just in case, I think we should have a new code. Three knocks means DANGER: COME AT ONCE.'

'Yes, OK. I just hope I don't sleep-walk again.'

'Don't worry about a thing. I'll be watching.'

It took me ages to go to sleep. My head was whirling with so many thoughts. Then the strangest thing happened. The meaning of that word *Glabula* burst into my head. I hadn't even been thinking about it either. I just sat up in bed and said to myself, 'It means "Come Home," doesn't it?'

'Now, why aren't you asleep yet?' Auntie Judy

was in the doorway. She was wearing her pale red dressing-gown.

'I've just remembered what *Glabula* means.'

She froze. 'Have you?'

'It means, "Come home", but I'm still not sure what language it is. And why would anyone write that as a message and stick it inside a book?'

'I don't know,' murmured Auntie Judy. 'Anyway, don't think about it any more tonight.'

But the word kept dancing around in my head.

Finally, I drifted off to sleep for a while. When I opened my eyes again, Auntie Judy was still there in the doorway, watching over me like a sentry.

I tried to mumble something to her. But then I was asleep once more. The next time I opened my eyes I was back at the scene of the accident.

He was waiting there for me.

This time he wasn't alone.

# CHAPTER TWELVE
## *by Sam*

I twisted my head sharply and saw them both standing in the half-darkness: him, and Aunt Margaret. Her face had lost some of its sharpness. She was looking at me pleadingly.

The man raised a hand to me. A hand with only three fingers. 'Glabula,' he said.

I looked up at him. 'Come home,' I said. 'It means "Come home", doesn't it?'

It was my aunt who replied. She leant forward. Her breath touched my cheek. She spoke to me using strange words I'd never heard before. Then he joined in. They went on and on. And I didn't understand anything. I was completely lost.

Until somewhere in the back of my head came this whispering. It was as if an interpreter was explaining the meaning of each word to me, but very quietly. Then all at once it was just like the volume on a radio being turned right up.

Suddenly my head was flooded with words, meanings . . . and memories. It was as if hundreds of doors which had been locked and barred to me had sprung open together, and I was running madly through each one.

I uttered a few words in that language. Aunt Margaret was positively beaming at me, so was the man. And now I saw he didn't have black eyes at all. No, they were a deep, purply blue, with glimmers of other colours in them too. And they were really bright, as if they'd just been polished.

He went on speaking to me in a language that wasn't strange and foreign any more. I could follow most of what he said now. He said I could touch his eyes if I wanted to. So I did. They felt amazingly soft. Touching eyes was our greeting. It was all coming back. I felt so happy, so triumphant. Excitement flooded through me.

And then I looked around and saw I was back in my bedroom again. I lay there, unable to believe what I'd found out. It was the most amazing discovery of all time. Just wait until I told Freddie. I threw off the blankets. This room was scorching hot tonight. I opened a window and got back into bed.

But I became even hotter. I was burning up inside. My face was smothered in sweat. And then I realized what was happening. My dream must have been so powerful I had started to . . . it happens sometimes . . . my hands shook under the covers. I lay there in the darkness, waiting.

My stomach gave a lurch. This was always the bit I hated most. Your insides just go haywire. And shivers run all over your skin. But it only ever lasts for a few seconds.

Suddenly my right arm became so hot I could see right through it. And then it began to melt slowly away like an ice-cream on a hot day. Soon all that was left of it was a pale smudge. Moments later, it had vanished completely.

Already my left arm was twitching uncertainly, as

if it knew it would be next. It started to dwindle away too. It didn't hurt: I had no feeling there at all except for a very slight itchiness. The burning feeling travelled down to my feet next. They slipped off me as easily as any shoe.

Then things speeded up as if the darkness was growing impatient; it hungrily gobbled up my chest, my tummy and legs, leaving just my face lying all by itself on the pillow.

If someone came in now! I wanted to smile but I couldn't because my mouth and nose had just fallen off me the way leaves fall off a tree. At the same time my skin was withering and growing more ancient by the second.

Finally, all that remained of me was a pile of clothes on the carpet, and two eyes.

My eyelids fluttered and flew away like small, hot butterflies. And now my eyes began to fade into the darkness too.

I was mouldering away to nothing . . . I was as tiny and insubstantial as a piece of dust. Yet, I was still here. I was still here!

Then came a huge rush of air as my new eyes formed out of the darkness. Then I felt myself being pulled and stretched, and squeezed like a piece of plasticine being sculpted into a new shape. This part was always so fast. Afterwards I lay there feeling breathless and giddy. My body felt as if it were being tickled by a feather. New clothes were sprouting.

Then, my shape-change was over.

I stretched forward to put on the light. Only I didn't need to stretch. My new hand could reach the switch easily now.

I got out of bed and tottered forward on legs which didn't quite belong to me yet.

I stood in front of the mirror on my dressing-table with my eyes shut.

I was scared of the ugly monster I'd see staring back at me. A shudder ran through me. I stood there for such a long time before I plucked up my courage.

At last I squinted open one eye. I took in an alien figure. My head was enormous, much larger than a human's. But it was kind of impressive too. My eyes were huge too: a lively deep, purply blue colour, with flashes of other colours darting in and out. I thought they looked stunning; I was proud of them. Shame my hair was so wispy but still, I had a perfect complexion; my pale, grey skin didn't have one spot.

My body was quite tall and thin and encased in a rather smart silver jumpsuit. I peered down at my feet: tiny, of course, with no toes. But what's so great about toes anyway?

My gaze returned to my eyes. I really did have some nice features. I wasn't a monster at all.

I opened both my eyes now and smiled at the creature in the mirror.

'Good to see you again,' I said.

## CHAPTER THIRTEEN
### by Sam

I started clapping my hands. I laughed. Now I understood the reason for all those spooky events.

And it was as if a great weight had been lifted from me. I rushed around the room. I couldn't keep still. I was so excited.

Then I just seemed to take off and fly right through my bedroom door. I didn't feel a thing either, except for a low humming in my ears. I tell you, it's the only way to travel. I floated down the stairs, brushing against the plants in the hallway and carried right on into the kitchen.

Sitting at the table were Auntie Judy and Aunt Margaret. I came crashing down to earth when I saw them. They both got up at once.

'Oh, hello love,' said Auntie Judy as if it was the most ordinary thing in the world for me to float through the kitchen door like this in the middle of the night. 'Don't you look splendid.' She kissed me on the cheek. 'I knew you'd remember, if they'd only let you alone and didn't keep pushing you so hard with all these stunts.'

'But Sam's memory might not have come back for weeks, or months. Swift action was needed.' Aunt Margaret turned to me. 'I'm so very pleased you've recovered.' Then she said gravely, 'I've been very anxious about you. You were due home three weeks ago, you know.'

'Yes, I know,' I began.

'You remember what happened just before your accident?'

'I think so. We quarrelled, didn't we?'

'We certainly did,' said Aunt Margaret. 'Your six months on Earth was over. But you wanted to stay longer, begged me for six more months, said you wanted to stay until Christmas. No-one has ever asked to stay longer here before.' She wrinkled up her nose. 'The idea of one of our people wishing to remain in such an infantile state . . .' She stretched out a hand to Auntie Judy. 'I don't mean to be rude, but it would be rather like an earthling living among the apes for a while, then wishing to remain an ape. Extraordinary.'

Auntie Judy didn't reply at first, then said gently, 'Well, I thought Sam made a very good human. Have you enjoyed it here on Earth, love?'

'Oh yes, it was just the best time,' I replied, softly. Auntie Judy and I smiled at each other.

'I hope you don't mind me asking, Auntie Judy,' I continued, 'but you're not an alien, are you?'

'Sam!' roared Aunt Margaret.

'I'm sorry,' I began.

'You know we never use the term alien; we are *cosmics*,' cried Aunt Margaret.

'Yes, of course, but there are still a few holes in my memory.'

'And that's quite natural. Memory is not a thing which can be rushed, as I've said more than once over these past days and nights.' Auntie Judy directed a stern look at Aunt Margaret. 'And no, I'm not a cosmic, love. But I've always enjoyed meeting people from other countries – and other planets too. I've been a contactee for some years now. There are lots of us, some in very key places in society. But we are pledged to secrecy. Because there are still many human beings who refuse to believe . . .'

'Only earthlings could think they have a whole universe to themselves,' said Aunt Margaret with a mirthless laugh.

Auntie Judy went on. 'So your Uncle Tony and I are honoured to be contactees and help a little . . . you're not the first cosmic to stay here with us, you know.'

'Arnold,' I cried, looking across at that one unsmiling face among the photos on the kitchen wall.

'That's right,' said Auntie Judy. 'He was, like you, very clever. But he just couldn't socialize. He would shuffle past people looking at his feet, never saying a word. Tony and I tried so hard to make him welcome but he was just homesick the whole time . . .'

'That's why,' interrupted Aunt Margaret, 'the next child on our Earth Experience Scheme had to be very carefully prepared. We spent months with you, working on your biography, doing everything to ensure you fitted in.' She sighed. 'And in the end you fitted in too well. You forgot you were sent on Earth to study earthlings and add to our collective understanding of them. You let us all down the day you demanded six more months here.'

I hung my head guiltily.

'These last few days have been such a trial for me,' continued Aunt Margaret. 'Nothing like this has ever happened before. If it hadn't been for Dr Willoughby, one of our senior cosmics . . .'

'Is that the man in my dreams?'

'Yes. After our quarrel I consulted him. I was with him when I heard about your accident. I let him go ahead of me. He tried to talk to you telepathically. A basic skill for every cosmic. When you couldn't communicate back, we knew how serious your situation was . . .'

'But why did you say Dr Willoughby wasn't there at the accident?' I asked.

'I had to protect his identity,' replied Aunt Margaret. 'But ever since, Dr Willoughby's been tapping into your dreams to try and trigger your memory.'

'Did he also arrange the sighting of the spacecraft?'

'Of course; we were absolutely certain that would set off some memories. Dr Willoughby has tried everything these last days . . . He's waiting in the garden now. May I invite him in?'

'Certainly,' said Auntie Judy. 'I had no idea he was out there.'

'Oh, he's been out there every night, waiting.'

Then he was in the kitchen, stretching out a hand to me. But it was a human hand again. As if reading my thoughts he said, 'Only my eyes remain cosmic now. I'd thought seeing the cosmic hand might jolt a few memories – and our salute too. But in the end it was one word on a card that did it.' He was speaking in cosmic to me until Auntie Judy gave a cough.

He immediately apologized. 'I'm so sorry,' he said to Auntie Judy. 'It was very rude of me to speak in our language – and I am sorry for the shock tactics we had to use on you, young lady. But for a while your mind had shut down, locking away your true identity. You might say we had to unlock your mind. Still, it is good to see you're yourself again – and now we must leave.'

'Leave?' I cried.

'Yes, of course. We have a long journey ahead of us.' He smiled politely at Auntie Judy. 'About four hundred million of your miles.' He returned to me. 'You've caused a great many problems, Samantha. It won't take you long to pack, will it?'

'No, it won't.' I spoke very quietly but inside my head I was screaming. I didn't want to go like this. Not now. And what about Freddie?

'Well, Sam, I expect you're looking forward to coming home,' said Dr Willoughby.

'Yes,' I replied, in an even quieter voice.

'You'd better go and shape-change back into your earthling form first,' he said. 'We don't want to alarm any earthlings.'

I nodded, but didn't move.

He and Aunt Margaret looked at me questioningly. I turned to Auntie Judy. 'Freddie,' I whispered.

But it was Aunt Margaret who answered. 'It's best we leave without disturbing that particular earthling.'

'But I can't,' I gasped.

'They're very close,' said Auntie Judy.

'I am aware of that,' replied Aunt Margaret, 'but I can see no good purpose in waking him now. He's a very uncontrollable boy at the best of times, and this event will only provoke him further. Who knows what he might do?'

'But . . .' I began.

Aunt Margaret gave me one of her looks. Cosmic children were never supposed to argue with their elders. Yet I just couldn't leave without seeing Freddie once more. I decided I'd go upstairs and make a noise. But then there was no need.

Freddie was already creeping downstairs. My heart leapt excitedly. Aunt Margaret heard him too. She immediately looked for guidance to Dr Willoughby. But there was no time for him to speak. Freddie was at the door.

I felt suddenly shy, and moved away into the corner. Freddie's attention was caught by Aunt Margaret – and Dr Willoughby. They stood in front of him, like two bodyguards.

Freddie pointed at Aunt Margaret. 'Auntie Judy, what's she doing here? And him? Who is he?' Then answering his own question. 'He's the man that Sam saw. Auntie Judy, we've got to protect her. She's not in her room again. I just looked.'

'Freddie, I'm here,' I whispered. He started. He stared into the corner of the kitchen. 'And you were right, aliens have only got three fingers.' I stretched out a hand to him.

He drew back. 'Sam, what are they doing to you?' His voice cracked.

I slowly turned round. I smiled at him. 'It's all right, Freddie, honestly,' I said softly.

His mouth opened without any words being said. Then he let out a bleat of terror, and hurtled forward.

# CHAPTER FOURTEEN
*by Freddie*

A shadow stirred. A hand appeared out of the darkness. It touched my face. The breath tore at my throat. The shadow moved again, assumed an identity. 'Auntie Judy,' I cried, 'what have they done to Sam?'

'It's all right, calm down, love,' whispered Auntie Judy. 'How do you feel?'

'Oh, I'm all right,' I replied, trying to sit up in bed. 'But Sam . . .'

Auntie Judy sat down on the bed beside me. 'Sam's just fine. And they haven't done anything to her. They've just been trying to help her . . . in their own way.'

'But what are you saying? Has Sam turned into some kind of alien?'

'The proper term is "cosmic". And yes, Sam is a cosmic. She always has been.'

'But she never looked like one before.'

'Cosmics can shape-change.' Auntie Judy gave a wry little smile. 'Surely an expert like you knows that.'

'But I still don't understand . . . how was she here?'

'She was chosen to come to Earth, quite an honour, actually. She's only the second cosmic child to make the trip. She was here to find out about us, only she liked us so much she didn't want to go back. She was starting to forget she was a cosmic even before the accident – of course afterwards she forgot everything about her cosmic life.'

'So all those weird events were for her benefit?'

Auntie Judy nodded.

'Bit grim, weren't they?'

'I told them that,' said Auntie Judy. 'But I'm only a lowly earthling. What do I know?' She lowered her voice: 'Cosmics aren't used to their plans going wrong, unlike us.' She patted my hand.

'And what's Sam doing now?'

'She's packing,' said Auntie Judy, quietly.

I looked up. 'But she can't just go.'

'They think it's for the best,' said Auntie Judy. 'I

shall be very sorry to see her go too.'

'No.' I struggled out of bed. I made it to the door. There I was met by Miss West.

She glowered down at me. 'I'd like to have a word with you, Freddie.'

'I want to see Sam first,' I demanded, trying to push past her.

But then that man I'd seen downstairs loomed in front of me again. He stared over my head at Auntie Judy. 'Perhaps you will be kind enough to see how Sam is getting on with her packing?' I sensed Auntie Judy stiffen.

'No harm will come to the young earthling,' he murmured. Somehow, I didn't like the way he said that.

But Auntie Judy said, 'Get back into bed, Freddie. I won't be long.'

'I want to see Sam,' I cried.

'Don't worry, you will,' she murmured.

I sat up in bed. I put on the light. The two figures seemed to take over the room completely, dwarfing all the pretend aliens on my shelves.

'You're both aliens, aren't you?' I was shouting because I was scared.

'We are proud to call ourselves cosmics,' said the man. 'Miss West, you know. I am Dr Willoughby.'

'Well, don't try and abduct me.'

He laughed as if I'd made a joke. 'We undertake very few abductions, as you call them. We'd much rather observe you earthlings in your natural habitat. You see, we know how to avoid all violence. Perhaps one day you earthlings will, too. That is why we are here, to understand how your minds work and one day soon, to teach you what we have learnt.'

'How to change the body you don't like for another one, you mean,' I said.

Miss West tut-tutted. 'We don't encourage such activities. Shape-change is a skill young children learn and we let them experiment with it for a while . . . it encourages children to use their brain. Did you know earthlings only use ten per cent of their brains?'

'As much as that?' I replied, sarcastically.

'We cosmics use seventy per cent of our brains, but our minds are capable of still more. That is our next goal . . .'

She went on speaking, but I was too busy listening to another sound: three knocks coming from the wall next door. Sam and I had said three knocks meant danger, hadn't we?

'It's been great talking to you,' I began, 'but I've got to go.'

Dr Willoughby raised his hand. 'Allow us just a few more moments of your time.' He was like a polite, but very pushy door-to-door salesman.

Three knocks pounded on the wall again. 'What's that?' demanded Miss West. 'Some kind of silly game.'

'I must go,' I repeated.

Dr Willoughby's face loomed right up in front of mine now. He was leaning in so close I could count the hairs up his nose.

His voice dropped very low. 'On our planet, Freddie, there are no wars, no disputes, no fighting . . . you have nothing to fear from us. We have everything to fear from you. For an earthling's first impulse is to destroy anyone different from themselves. Yet, we continue to infiltrate your society, doing so many good things undetected. That is why, Freddie, we have to, regretfully, do this to you . . .'

'Do what to me?' I gasped.

I knew I should stop looking at Dr Willoughby. But his deep, black eyes were like a magnet and kept pulling me back. I couldn't get away. I was caught, trapped. I could feel myself draining away.

'I've come to say goodbye to Freddie.'

Sam's voice jolted me back to life. For a moment there I'd been drifting off to sleep. 'Auntie Judy said it would be all right,' she continued.

'Have you finished your packing?' asked Miss West.

'Just about.'

'Just about,' repeated Miss West. 'What kind of imprecise answer is that? You really have been among earthlings far too long.'

But then Dr Willoughby tapped Miss West on the shoulder as if to say, it's all right for them to say goodbye. So Miss West said, 'Be quick, please,' and left. Dr Willoughby gave me a little bow. He seemed a bit too pleased with himself for my liking.

Usually Sam just sank down on to my chair in the corner. Today she hovered, looking awkward. Neither of us knowing quite what to say.

'Well, that was an amazing costume you put on downstairs,' I joked. 'Fooled me completely.'

She gave a shaky little laugh. We'd never been more shy with each other, not even on the day when we first met.

'You signalled our code for danger,' I said.

'Yes.' I looked at her questioningly. 'It was you I was worried about,' began Sam. 'Did Dr Willoughby get you to stare into his eyes?'

'Well, he plonked his face right up to mine, if that's what you mean?'

She gave a little cry of distress.

'What's wrong? Tell me,' I demanded.

'I'm too late,' she whispered.

'Too late?'

'He was trying to send you to sleep.'

'Miss West is the expert at that; she sends me into a small coma every time she speaks.'

But Sam didn't smile. 'This is totally different, Freddie. What he's done is . . . If you fall asleep in the next few minutes, then when you wake up you'll have forgotten everything about tonight. Actually, they might be playing it really safe and . . .' She hesitated.

'Go on.'

'When you wake up you won't remember me at all. So stay awake. I want to be remembered.' She gave another shaky little laugh. 'The first sign that it's working is you have this kind of mild headache.'

With a stab of alarm I realized I did have a headache: the kind you get just after you've eaten too much ice-cream too quickly. I scrambled out of bed. Maybe it would help if I walked around a bit. I paced up and down and took some deep breaths. 'I think his spell might be working a little on me, but don't worry.' I turned and looked at her. 'I'm staying awake all tonight.'

'Thought you might prefer to forget tonight, especially after what you saw in the kitchen. Never seen you faint before.'

'Not something I usually do actually, but it was just . . .'

'A big shock.'

'That's right. I mean, even aliens have got more hair than me. I still can't believe that.'

She half-laughed. 'You never guessed that I was one.'

'No, you kept that secret well.'

'So well that I forgot it myself for a while.'

'And you can change back into an alien whenever you want?'

'I can change into anyone I want.'

'Decent.'

'But we're not encouraged to do much changing. We're all supposed to look the same, and dress the same. It makes life less complicated.'

'I suppose.' My legs were starting to feel alarmingly heavy. I tottered forward.

'Sit down for a bit,' said Sam.

'No, better keep moving.' I took some more deep breaths. 'Keep talking to me, Sam. So what's alien-land like then? Miss West said there's never any wars or fighting.'

'That's true. We don't have any parents either.'

'What?'

'We have specially trained guardians who are entrusted to look after us. They think it stops all the emotional problems you get on earth.'

'So Miss West isn't really your aunt?'

'Oh, no.'

'That's one bit of good news then.'

'We don't have music either, or films or video, or books with stories in them. And we don't have Halloween or Guy Fawkes or Christmas.'

'You don't have Christmas!'

'No, it's like January all the time there. That's why I loved to read about the Earth. Earth Studies is my best subject actually.' She smiled shyly. 'I'd spend hours and hours imagining it all down here, and especially Christmas.'

From downstairs came Miss West's voice. 'Sam, we're ready to leave now.'

Sam looked at me.

'Don't go,' I said.

'I don't want to – but I've no choice. I have to obey.'

I tried to say something else but instead I slumped down onto the bed.

Sam knelt down beside me. 'And you're going to fall asleep and forget everything I've just told you, aren't you?'

I just managed to raise my head. 'No.'

'Yes you will, as soon as your eyelids close.' She got up. 'Goodbye, Freddie, I'll miss you more than I can say, and by the way, I don't think it would do any harm when your dad rings, if you give him a chance. But what's the point of me giving you advice, you'll have forgotten everything I said in the morning . . . you'll have forgotten me.'

'Stop saying that.' With a great effort I stumbled to my feet. 'Look, just tell Miss West or whoever she is that you want to stay until Christmas.'

'She won't listen.'

'All right, pretend you've lost your memory again.'

Sam considered this. Then she shook her head regretfully. 'No, I don't think that would work again.'

'Well, we'll just have to think of something else. There's got to be a way.'

Now it was Auntie Judy's voice calling up the stairs.

Sam's voice fell. 'There's no time. Come on, give me a goodbye hug then.'

'No, I won't. Because you're not going. I won't let you. I'll stop them.'

She gave a sad, little smile. 'Freddie, you can hardly stand up. What can you do?'

'What can I do?' I repeated. And that's when an amazing idea came speeding into my head. 'Listen,' I hissed, 'they think they've hypnotized me. I'll go downstairs and show them they've done no such thing. And I'll say if they won't let you stay until Christmas I'll tell everyone about aliens. I'll blow their cover. I'll tell the newspapers. I'll go on breakfast television . . .' Sam was staring at me, not saying a word. I rushed on. 'And Miss West will believe I'll do it. I mean, she'd believe anything about me, wouldn't she?' Sam nodded slowly. 'I'll make sure I don't stare into Dr Willoughby's eyes when I'm talking to him either. Well, go on, say something.'

'It might just work,' she whispered. 'Oh, Freddie, if I could stay here for a few more months with you . . .'

'Leave it to me.' I began to make slow steps to the door. Soon I was gasping for breath and I fell back onto the bed again.

'It's no good,' cried Sam, 'you'll never make it downstairs.' Then she stopped. 'But there is just one other way.'

# CHAPTER FIFTEEN
*by Freddie*

It was just a few seconds later and Sam was saying to me, 'Come on, Freddie, turn your head away.'

'Why?'

'Because you'll put me off if you don't. And we haven't got much time.'

There was no mistaking the urgency in her voice. This was our last hope.

'All right,' I said, lying back in bed. But I couldn't resist one peek. Sam was standing in the middle of the room. There was this kind of heat haze all around her.

And then her left arm vanished. It just spun off into the darkness. I let out a cry. I couldn't help it. It was horrible seeing someone's arm chopped off like that. In fact, it was disgusting.

'You're looking.'

'No, no.'

'Yes you are.'

'Sam, can I just ask: are you sure you know what you're doing?'

'Freddie, I've been shape-changing since I was two.'

'They let you shape-change at two. Well, I think that's really irresponsible. You wouldn't be allowed to do it here at two. You'd have to be ten, at least . . . So, does it hurt?'

'It does at first because your insides jump about a bit and you feel as if you're going to be sick. But once things start dropping off you feel much better.'

'I'll take your word for it. Now, where exactly has your arm gone?'

'What?'

'And are you sure you can get it back?'

'Freddie, stop asking silly questions. I need silence for this.'

That's what people say when they're about to do a magic trick. Well, this was the magic trick to end them all. I thought of something else. 'That day when you saw Dr Willoughby in the library and then he vanished, had he shape-changed into the caretaker?'

'Yes, he's a real expert. He can shape-change as quick as a flash. But I'm out of practice. It was strictly forbidden when I was an earthling. Also, I bet Dr Willoughby doesn't have someone breaking his concentration all the time.'

I didn't say another word. I closed my eyes, intending to rest them for a moment. The next thing I knew, a very familiar voice was whispering my name. I gazed up and saw . . . ME.

'What do you think of me now?' asked Sam.

'A distinct improvement,' I quipped. But really, it was the weirdest experience; it was just as if my reflection had hopped out of the mirror and was now in front of me in all its three dimensions. I found myself gazing at the back of my head. I'd never really seen it before. I hadn't missed much.

'Even your voice is just like mine,' I said, 'but haven't you made me a bit short?'

'No, this is exactly how you are, even down to the clothes you were wearing tonight. Now, when you walk, you do this kind of swagger, don't you?'

'Yeah, it's a cool person's swagger.'

'In your dreams,' teased Sam.

Then we both froze. The stairs creaked. Someone was coming up the stairs. 'We've no more time,' hissed Sam. 'Look, if this doesn't work . . .'

'It's got to,' I said, firmly.

'But if it doesn't, I probably won't see you again. Don't worry, though, I'll get back in contact.'

'I'll keep watching the skies.' I said this as a kind of joke but then I whispered, 'I'll be watching all right.' I got out of bed. We shook hands. 'First time I've ever shaken hands with myself,' I said. 'You know it should be me doing this.'

She smiled. 'It will be you.'

Then I whispered sharply, 'Look!' I was pointing at the crack under the door. I could see a shape moving about there. A moment later the door handle turned. But the door didn't open because Sam was putting all her weight against it.

'Lock it,' I hissed.

'Oh, yes.' Sam slammed on the bolt at the top of the door.

My door handle rattled and shook.

'Open the door at once.' It was Miss West. 'We're all waiting for you, Sam.'

'She won't be a minute,' I said. 'We're just saying goodbye.'

'How long does it take to say goodbye?' muttered Miss West. She sounded as if she were speaking through clenched teeth.

Sam whispered to me, 'As soon as the coast is clear I'll spring out and say Sam is too upset to come down. Lock the door behind me, and if anyone starts knocking on the door don't say anything, just cry.'

'Cry!' I exclaimed.

'Yes, make a few sobbing noises. You can do it, Freddie.'

'Sure I can. Don't let Dr Willoughby try and hypnotize you, will you?'

'Don't worry, I'll be careful.'

I sat down again on the bed.

'She's still right outside the door,' said Sam. 'I can see her prowling about.'

But then, at last, Miss West did move away.

'Here we go,' whispered Sam.

I hauled myself up again. Quickly, but very quietly, Sam opened the door. Immediately, I closed and locked the door behind her, then I stood listening.

Miss West was saying, 'Sam really has got to leave now. I suggest you retire to your bedroom, Freddie, you must be very sleepy by now.'

'Actually, I've never felt more awake,' replied a well-loved voice. 'You see, your little plot to hypnotize me didn't work, and unless you want me to shout out everything I know about you and that Dr Willoughby, I suggest we have a little talk downstairs right now.'

'What nonsense is this?' She turned the door handle, then banged on my bedroom door. 'Sam, open this door at once.'

I started to make what I hoped sounded like crying noises. Actually, I think I sounded more like a retarded guinea pig. I threw in quite a few sniffs too. I was good at doing those.

Then 'Freddie' said to Miss West, 'It's no good. She won't come out, so please listen to what I've got to say. Otherwise, I'm going to cause you a great deal of trouble.'

I could imagine Miss West giving him one of her evil stares but then she said, 'I can give you two minutes only, Freddie.' She called in to me, 'I am taking your case downstairs. And I want you downstairs at once, Sam. If it weren't for your recent problems I would be very angry with you. You're still behaving like an earthling, not a cosmic.'

I stayed, crouched against the door, listening to Sam downstairs. She was great as ME. Better than the original, in fact. Then the adults piped up. They were speaking quite loudly at first, but all at once their voices faded. I had to strain to hear anything. Was this a good sign? I could only hope.

I crawled back to bed. My eyes felt really heavy. So did my insides. Yet I hadn't eaten a thing this evening. It was my tiredness which was making me feel so full. But I wouldn't go to sleep.

I kept looking all around my room. My army of aliens were in their usual place along the shelf. To keep myself awake I whispered softly to them,

'Tonight, three real aliens have been in here. They're certainly far more advanced than us, but their lives aren't that great, you know.'

The models stared back at me as if eager to hear more. 'They don't seem to have much fun, and they're very serious. Imagine a planet full of Miss Wests. No thanks . . . and they don't have any families. Not even parents. That's good, it means you never have any mums walking out on you . . . or dads sending you stupid letters.'

I stopped. My dad's picture still lay, face-down, on my bedside table. I picked it up and stared into the photograph. I thought he might look different after what he'd told me in his letter. But he didn't. He was still smiling away while looking into the distance.

When he next called, did I want to talk to him? In a way, I did. Yet, once I spoke to him he'd be back in my life. I'd be giving him the power to hurt me again. I lay there, thinking and thinking what to do.

Finally, I put the picture back on the dressing-table – but not face-down this time. Downstairs I heard ME cry out, 'I shall start by asking Miss West how you ever got a job at my school? You may be from a superior race but I doubt if you've got any of our qualifications. You must have a contactee: someone very high up in the educational world.

Well, I'm going to blow that person's cover, and all your other contactees.' A moment later 'Freddie' piped up again, 'You say I'm not being fair. Is it fair for aliens to come down, become good friends with people like me, then just shoot off again without any explanation. You weren't even going to let Sam say goodbye to me. You cosmics have really messed my life up I can tell you.'

If I'd had the energy I'd have cheered. Sam was saying everything I wanted to say. It was uncanny. It was a new high in inter-galactic under-standing. We had to win.

I struggled so hard to stay awake. I kept squeezing my eyes open every time I wanted to drift off.

Then someone came rushing up the stairs.

'It's me,' hissed my voice. 'Open up.'

I got up and fumbled with the bolt. Sam sprang inside and bolted the door again.

'What an argument . . .' she said. 'You made some very good points, by the way.'

'Of course.'

'But I got them worried – or you did. Then Dr Willoughby came in on our side.'

'You're joking,' I cried.

'No, I was pretty amazed too. He thinks me staying here might promote a better understanding of earthlings – and so create harmony between our

138

planets. He rattled on for ages about it. Miss West took some persuading. But the great thing is, they've both agreed I can stay until the day after Boxing Day.'

I could hardly speak I was so happy.

'There's one condition though. You and I have to take the cosmic oath.'

'What's that when it's at home?'

'It means we swear we won't reveal anything about the cosmic world to any earthling. Cosmics do have to be very careful. So that's why we have to take the proper oath. And you might see a blue light on your forehead after you've taken the oath . . . that's a tracking device so they always know where you are. It's just another precaution.'

'Yeah, right.' But I hesitated. I wasn't sure I liked the idea of aliens knowing where I was at any time of night or day. It was as if they owned me. Suddenly I was their property.

'You don't have to do this,' said Sam.

But I did. 'Of course I'll do it,' I replied.

Sam's face lit up. 'But do you think you can manage to get downstairs?'

'No problem,' I said, even as sleep was tugging at my eyes again.

'Look, I'm going to shape-change next door. Can you get dressed into these clothes?' – she pointed at what she was wearing – 'really fast?'

'Just open a window for me, will you? A bit of fresh air might . . .'

'Sure.' She flung open the window and said, 'This is the last lap now, Freddie.'

'I know, and I won't let you down.'

She dashed into her room while I went over to the window. I took a couple of deep breaths, then staggered backwards. The fresh air didn't wake me up as I'd hoped. It just made me feel much worse.

The tiredness was like a terrible pain now. My head flopped down onto my chest.

And then I began to fall into darkness.

# CHAPTER SIXTEEN
*by Freddie*

I came round with a start.

A voice said, 'Don't move your head.'

I began to panic. Why shouldn't I move my head – and where was I? I squinted open my eyes. Sam, back in her earthling form, was crouched down and staring anxiously at me. 'Be careful,' she said, 'or you'll hit your head on the radiator.'

I looked up. A radiator towered above my head. Then I realized I was lying on the carpet. My bedroom looked really odd from this angle. It made me feel quite giddy. I blinked twice.

'Freddie, it's all right, you don't have to go downstairs,' said Sam. 'It's too much for you to do.'

My heart gave a horrible jolt. 'Don't be silly. I'll do it. I just passed out for a second. I feel much better now.' If only that were true. 'Come on, help me up.'

Frowning with concentration I got to my feet. There was no time for me to get dressed. So I just shoved on a dressing-gown — that took me ages — and then I began the journey downstairs, holding on tightly to Sam's arm as if I were a doddery old man. And with each step I seemed to grow even more ancient: ninety . . . ninety-one . . . ninety-two. I started counting. It kept me awake.

I'd reached one hundred and two when I saw Auntie Judy in the lounge. I have a feeling she knew I was struggling, because she said briskly, 'Now the children have been up quite late enough, so let's do this as quickly as possible, please.'

Sam gave my hand a squeeze, then I crawled to the other side of the room — it seemed acres away

– where Miss West and Dr Willoughby were waiting. I mustn't mess this up, I said fiercely to myself. I was as tense as a tightly wound spring.

'Are you all right, my boy?' asked Dr Willoughby. 'You look a little unsteady.'

'Never felt better,' I shouted. 'Now, what do I have to do?' I tell you, I was giving the performance of my life.

Dr Willoughby began spouting away. 'We are trusting you with a great secret, Freddie, one which you must never reveal to another earthling. If you do, you put in jeopardy not only the work of the cosmics, but their lives too. We do not use weapons any more but our bodies are as susceptible to them as earthlings . . . Careless talk costs cosmic lives.'

'Is that absolutely clear?' cut in Miss West.

I just glared at her as hard as I could.

Dr Willoughby continued. 'Sam will live here for the next six months as an earthling. She will never use her powers, nor will she ever refer to them. She is here only to learn, first-hand, about earthlings. Miss West is leaving tonight.'

A small smile formed on my face. I couldn't help it.

'A new guide will make herself known to Sam shortly. She will not be permitted to tell you who

143

it is, so please do not ask her. Your guide . . .'

'Mine?'

'Oh yes, you need a guide also. This is a fellow contactee who will make themselves known to you very soon. Your contactee will say the phrase "I'll be watching you" twice, that will be your password. Now, we must take the oath.'

At last, I thought. I was so exhausted I could hardly stand up. Dr Willoughby extended his hand. 'Do you take the oath of allegiance? You reply by saying, "Yes, I take the oath of allegiance".'

'Yes, I take the oath of allegiance.'

'Now place three fingers on my forehead as I put three fingers on yours.' He put three fingers onto my forehead. They felt really hot. I was about to copy him when Miss West chipped in, 'Remember, only three fingers,' and she was leaning over me just as she did at school.

'I know,' I muttered, twisting my little finger away. Then, all at once I jumped back with alarm.

'Don't move,' ordered Dr Willoughby.

'Sorry,' I mumbled. 'It's just I'd forgotten about the blue light.' Actually, it was more like lots of tiny blue flashes breaking out all over my forehead. They didn't exactly hurt, just made me feel as if I was about to sneeze. I didn't sneeze, but my nose kept on feeling really itchy and prickly.

Dr Willoughby took his fingers away from my forehead. 'Your skin will feel very tender there for a few days. But don't put any of your creams on it. They will only aggravate it. The skin will return to normal, leaving a very tiny pimple behind.'

Next it was Sam's turn to take the oath. I steadied myself against the chair. After that, I hardly remember going up the stairs again. In fact, the next thing I remember is waking up in the morning to see light bursting in through my curtains. The light seemed to fill my room.

My head was full of the strangest things: Sam turning into an alien — or cosmic. That was the word she'd used, then shape-changing into me.

Had it just been a crazy dream? It was so hard to know what was real and what wasn't. Sam would tell me. I got out of bed. My legs felt very shaky. I knocked twice on the wall. No answer. Was she still asleep? I stumbled next door.

She wasn't there and her room was practically

bare. Most of her things had gone.

'Sam,' I called. Silence.

I staggered back to my room. Had last night really happened? I had to work this out. I looked around me.

The aliens were all standing in exactly the same positions as usual. But something was different in this room. Then I saw what it was.

Last night my dad's picture had lain face-down. This morning he was smiling up at me once more. I must have moved the picture in the night. But why?

It was just the tiniest clue, but after that more and more parts of last night came flooding back to me, clearer than any dream ever could be. I darted a glance at myself in the mirror. The middle of my forehead was red and swollen; it looked as if it had caught a tiny bit of sunburn.

Then I knew it was all true.

And I really had helped to save Sam. But where

was she now? The house was eerily still. At the last moment had the cosmics seen through our plan and taken Sam away with them after all? I got out of bed again. I still felt a bit groggy. But I had to know if Sam was safe.

I half-ran, half-fell down the stairs. I opened the kitchen door. Sean was standing up, eating a piece of toast. He waved it at me. No-one else was about. 'I've been partying all night and I can still get up earlier than you.'

Normally I'd have given a funny reply in return, but today I just asked, 'Where's Sam?'

'She's around,' said Sean, vaguely.

'Where?'

He considered. 'She went for a walk with Auntie Judy. Yes, that's it. She's just had some good news. Her aunt said she can stay with us until Christmas. She said that will give her a chance to prepare their new home and for Sam to get used to the idea.'

I got up. 'So have they gone to the common?'

'I expect so. But chat with me first. Here, have some toast, nice and burnt.' He flung me a piece. 'I'm off to my Saturday job soon. Try and stay out of trouble while I'm away, won't you. Remember, I'll be watching you.'

The toast nearly fell out of my hands. *I'll be watching you*. I'd been told those were the words my guide would use. But Sean? It must just be a coincidence.

'I'll be watching you,' said Sean again. Then he grinned at my startled face. 'Yes, I'm your cosmic tour guide.'

'But you don't even believe in aliens,' I exclaimed.

'I felt bad about saying that,' said Sean. 'My instructions were to put you off the scent. But now they've decided you can be trusted,' he grinned. 'Not that you left them much choice.'

'How long have you been a . . . ?'

'A contactee. Three years.'

'And you've never told anyone?'

'No, I'm not even supposed to talk about it with Auntie Judy or Uncle Tony. Careless talk costs cosmic lives, you know. Still, it's quite an honour to be chosen. It's a shock when you first find out though, isn't it?'

I smiled and nodded.

'I caught Arnold doing a spot of shape-changing. Poor Arnold, got a right ear-bashing afterwards. Still, I've proved earthlings can keep the greatest secret in the world and so will you, with a little help from your friendly cosmic guide.'

I heard the front door open. I rushed into the hall. Sean followed. I saw Sam disappearing upstairs. Auntie Judy was smiling at me.

'Freddie and I have just been having a bit of a chat, Auntie Judy,' said Sean. 'I told him about Sam staying until Christmas now.'

'Yes. Life's just full of surprises, isn't it,' said Auntie Judy. There was a definite twinkle in her eyes as she said this.

'Can I see Sam now?' I asked.

'Of course you can,' said Auntie Judy. 'I know she'll want to see you. She's in her room, unpacking.'

I raced upstairs. Sam's door was half-open. She heard me and turned round.

'We did it, Freddie,' she said. Then she took hold of my hand and held it, just as she had when I was stumbling down the stairs last night.

'Six whole months here,' she whispered. And she was staring around her as if she'd just been given a million birthday presents all at once.

'I know we're not supposed to talk,' I whispered, 'but there's so much I want to ask you. I mean, I don't even know the name of your planet, or how long it took you to get here, or what it's like travelling in a spaceship, or . . .'

'Maybe one day you'll find out.'

I stared at her.

'I want you to come back with me, Freddie, for a visit.'

'Try and stop me,' I gasped.

'I can't say any more now, walls have ears and all that. But when we're alone on the common . . .'

'Sitting on top of the slide.'

'That's right.' She smiled. 'There's so much I want to tell you, Freddie.'

'I'll bet — and believe me, I want to hear it.' I sighed. 'I mean. I've read so much about UFOs and aliens; watched every film and TV programme about them . . . but now I'll get all the inside information, know the truth from the alien, sorry, cosmic, in my house. Don't be surprised if my head explodes with excitement, will you?'

'It had better not. I've got so much still to see on Earth too,' she said.

'I know. And believe me you're not going to miss a thing. In fact, I think we should make a list right now.'

That's exactly what we did. Soon the list was longer than any homework I'd ever done. Auntie Judy brought us up some tea and toast, but I still carried on writing. We were putting down silly things now. I loved the way that list kept growing.

I never heard the phone ring. I just heard Auntie Judy calling up the stairs, 'Freddie, it's your dad. He'd like a word.'

I sort of seized up. It was like the night I saw that UFO. I stood there, glued to the spot. I couldn't even answer.

I think Auntie Judy realized this because she said, 'Well, I'll be chatting to your dad for a bit, so pop down if you want.'

I stared at Sam. 'I didn't think he'd ring this early.'

'He must be keen.'

'It's probably a cheap rate now, or something. Parents, who needs them? Superior races don't bother with them. And they should know, shouldn't they?'

Sam didn't answer.

I sighed. 'No, it's best I don't speak to him. That

way there's no chance of him letting me down, or any more hassle.'

She half-turned away. 'No chance of anything good either,' she said, softly.

I stood thinking for a moment. Then I dived into my bedroom. I knew what Sam said was right, but I was dead scared too. I needed my alien mask. I picked it up off the floor. I gave it a quick dust, my hand shaking like crazy. I could always think better when I was wearing it.

Sam was hovering outside her bedroom. I was about to put the mask on. Instead, I flung it to her. She caught it easily. 'When you've seen the real thing,' I whispered, 'this looks a bit corny. Anyway, I'm going to . . . take my call.'

A smile spread across Sam's face.

'And Sam, I've got masses more things to add to our list. We've hardly started yet.'

Then I raced down the stairs, took the phone from Auntie Judy, drew two enormous breaths, and said, 'Hi, dad, how are you doing? It's me, Freddie.'

**THE END**

# THE GHOST DOG
## *by Pete Johnson*

*'I sensed hot breath on my neck. It was
right behind me. It'll get me, I must run faster . . .
faster . . .'*

Only mad scientists in stories can create
monsters, can't they? Not ten-year-old boys like
Daniel. Well, not until the night of his spooky
party when he and his friends make up a ghost
story about a terrifying dog . . .

It's a story made up to frighten Aaron – tough,
big-headed Aaron. But to Dan's horror, what
begins as a story turns into a nightmare. Each
night the ghost dog – a bloodthirsty, howling
monster – haunts his dreams, and Dan suspects
that what he conjured up with his imagination
has somehow become . . . real!

**'Compulsive readability'**
*The Junior Bookshelf*

**'Incredibly enjoyable . . . an exciting and
touching story about friendship and the power of
imagination, especially that of a child'**
*Books for Keeps*

WINNER OF THE 1996 YOUNG TELEGRAPH/FULLY
BOOKED AWARD

WINNER OF THE 1997 STOCKTON CHILDREN'S BOOK OF THE
YEAR AWARD

ISBN 0 440 86341 4

# MY FRIEND'S A WEREWOLF
## *by Pete Johnson*

*Now I know for certain Simon is a werewolf!*

Kelly always thought werewolves only existed in stories and late-night films. Until Simon moves in next door. Kelly and Simon become instant friends, but Kelly just can't help noticing that there's something very odd about her new friend. For one thing he wears black gloves all the time – even at school. And could that be hair starting to sprout on his face? Last, but definitely not least, there's the howling at night . . .

Aren't werewolves . . . dangerous?

**'A howling good read'**
*Young Telegraph*

**'The horrors build up nicely to a climax'**
*Books for Keeps*

**'Has the tension, the fear of the known and unknown plus a gradual build-up to a climax apparently typical of the genre, yet that climax is not only gripping but both unexpected and convincing . . . A really compelling tale'**
*Carousel*

ISBN 0 440 86342 2

# THE PHANTOM THIEF
## *by Pete Johnson*

*YOU ARE IN DANGER . . .*

The first time Alfie sees the boy, he appears
as if from nowhere in the school detention
room – the 'padded cell'. There's something
odd about him and Alfie is definitely not
pleased when he realizes the boy has nicked
his new jacket. But a ghost? His new friend
Sarah is convinced – so convinced she is
prepared to ghost-watch with him. And
that's when the warning message appears,
scratched out on the blackboard by
a phantom hand . . .

ISBN 0 440 86370 8

# CLOCKWORK
## or
# ALL WOUND UP
### *by Philip Pullman*

*Tick, tock, tick, tock! Some stories are like that. Once you've wound them up, nothing will stop them . . .*

A tormented apprentice clock-maker – and a deadly knight in armour. A mechanical prince – and the sinister Dr Kalmenius, who some say is the devil . . . Wind up these characters, fit them into a story on a cold winter's evening, with the snow swirling down, and suddenly life and the story begin to merge in a peculiarly macabre – and unstoppable – way.

Almost like clockwork . . .

**'Exciting, scary, romantic and deliciously readable'**
*The Guardian*

SILVER MEDAL WINNER,
SMARTIES AWARD IN 1997

SHORTLISTED FOR THE
CARNEGIE MEDAL IN 1997

ISBN 0 440 86343 0

# JACQUELINE HYDE
*by Robert Swindells*

*'I was bursting with energy, ready for anything. For the first time in my life, I was alive. Fully alive.'*

Jacqueline Hyde has always been a *good* girl. But from the moment she finds the little glass bottle in Grandma's attic, Jacqueline's life changes. Suddenly she's cheeky and loud, in with the roughest gang at school – Jacqueline *Bad*.

It's fun at first. Exciting. But then Jacqueline Bad gets into *serious* trouble. And although she keeps *trying* to be her old self, the bad side just won't let go . . .

**'Utterly believable . . . the breathless, short chapters make page turning unavoidable'**
*Junior Bookshelf*

ISBN 0 440 86329 5

All Corgi Yearling titles are available by post from:

Book Service By Post, PO Box 29,
Douglas, Isle of Man, IM99 1BQ

Credit cards accepted.
Please telephone 01624 675137, fax 01624 670923
or Internet http://www.bookpost.co.uk
or e-mail: bookshop@enterprise.net for details

Free postage and packing in the UK.
Overseas customers: allow £1 per book (paperbacks)
and £3 per book (hardbacks)